MALLORY AND THE
TROUBLE WITH TWINS

**Other books by
Ann M. Martin**

Rachel Parker, Kindergarten Show-off
Eleven Kids, One Summer
Ma and Pa Dracula
Yours Turly, Shirley
Ten Kids, No Pets
Slam Book
Just a Summer Romance
Missing Since Monday
With You and Without You
Me and Katie (the Pest)
Stage Fright
Inside Out
Bummer Summer

BABY-SITTERS LITTLE SISTER series
THE BABY-SITTERS CLUB mysteries
THE BABY-SITTERS CLUB series

THE BABY-SITTERS CLUB

MALLORY AND THE TROUBLE WITH TWINS

Ann M. Martin

AN
APPLE
PAPERBACK

SCHOLASTIC INC.
New York Toronto London Auckland Sydney

This book is for
the Palladinos
and the Ameses,
especially Kathy.

Cover art by Hodges Soileau

No part of this publication may be reproduced in whole or in part, or stored in a retrieval system, or transmitted in any form or by any means, electronic, mechanical, photocopying, recording, or otherwise, without written permission of the publisher. For information regarding permission, write to Scholastic Inc., 555 Broadway, New York, NY 10012.

ISBN 0-590-67389-0

12 11 10 9 8 7 6 5   2   0 1/0

Printed in the U.S.A.   40

CHAPTER 1

"Kindergarten baby, stick your head in gravy! Wash it off with applesauce and show it to the Navy!" sang Nicky.

"Mommy, make him stop!" cried Claire.

"Nicholas Pike," said my mother, "this is supposed to be fun. We are going to Washington Mall, which you have been begging to do for weeks, and where, I might add, each of you kids is going to get a new pair of shoes. You do want new shoes, don't you?"

"Yes," said Nicky contritely.

"Then apologize to your sister. She doesn't like being called a kindergarten baby. You didn't like it either when you were her age."

"Sorry, Claire," said Nicky.

Mom didn't see it, because we were so jam-packed into our car, but Claire's response was to stick her tongue out at Nicky. So he silently mouthed "kindergarten baby" to her and she turned bright red. If I hadn't grabbed her then,

1

who knows what would have happened?

There are eight kids in my family. Nicky and Claire are just two of them, but they were having a big enough fight for all of us.

I am Mallory. I'm eleven and the oldest. Claire is five and the youngest. Between Claire and me are Margo, who's seven, Nicky, who's eight, Vanessa, who's nine, and the triplets, who are ten. The triplets are Adam, Byron, and Jordan, and they're identical. You would hardly know this, though, since they always wear different clothes and have such different personalities.

After I grabbed Claire, she calmed down. It was a good thing I was sitting between her and Nicky. I had put myself there on purpose. When it comes to kids — my brothers and sisters, or any others — I'm pretty smart. For instance, I had figured out the seating arrangement for our outing to the mall. (It takes awhile to drive there.) I had put Margo in the front seat with Mom and Dad, since she gets carsick sometimes and riding in the front is less bumpy. I had put the triplets in the way back, where they could be jerks without bothering anybody, especially Nicky, whom they are apt to tease mercilessly. And in the backseat, I had put Claire, me, Nicky, and Vanessa, in that order. Sitting between Claire and Nicky, I could break up fights. And with Vanessa by the window, she could daydream or make up poems, lost in her own world, which is how she's happiest.

"There's the mall!" cried Margo, pointing. She had survived the trip without once saying she was going to barf.

"All *right!*" cried Nicky. "New shoes. I want sneakers, and they have to be Reeboks. Or Avias. Either one."

"Oh, you are so cool, Nick," said Adam sarcastically from the back.

"Shut up!"

"*You* shut up!"

"Mom, Nicky and Adam said 'shut up,' " announced Claire.

"I heard," said Mom dryly. (Poor Mom. Since Dad was driving, she got stuck handling the squabbling and complaining.) "And all I have to say is this: How badly does any of you want shoes?"

Us kids "shut up" right away. We didn't think Mom would *really* not buy shoes for us . . . but we couldn't be sure. Long car rides with eight children could drive anyone crazy. (I should point out, by the way, that our mother is not an ogre. She's just human. And half an hour of kindergarten baby and tattling was wearing on her nerves.)

Dad pulled into the entrance to Washington

Mall and found a parking space that was about three miles away from the nearest store. We hiked over to a boutique, walked through it, and were in . . . the mall.

I swear, the mall is another world. You are surrounded by stores and shops, and even better things: food stands, exhibits, a flower mart, and my personal favorite, the ear-piercing boutique. I hardly know where to look.

As badly as we wanted new shoes, my brothers and sisters and I also wanted to be turned loose to go exploring.

But, "Shoes first," said Dad.

So we went to Antoinette's Shoe Tree (what on earth *is* a shoe tree?) and each got what we needed — *not*, I might emphasize, what we *wanted*. For example, what I wanted were these extremely cool pink shoes with green trim. What I got were loafers.

"They're much more practical," said Mom. "They go with almost everything you own. And they'll last at least a year."

When you are a parent of eight children, you have to think of these things. But when you are an eleven-year-old who has to show up in school every day, you just want those cool pink shoes.

As soon as we'd gotten our shoes, Mom and Dad let us kids split up so we could explore the mall for an hour. We had brought along spending money and were eager to, well, spend it. So the triplets went off by themselves, Nicky went off with Dad, Vanessa went off with Mom, and Claire and Margo begged to come with me.

"You do fun things," said Margo.

That was true. I check out all the stuff I'm not allowed to have yet, like glitter for my hair, makeup, and short skirts.

"Today," I announced, "we're going to watch people have their ears pierced."

"Goody," said Claire, and we set off.

The mall is huge, but I could find my way to the ear-piercing boutique blindfolded, so we reached it in under two minutes.

A girl my age was sitting on a stool, about to have a hole made in her right ear. I noticed that she already had one hole in each ear, and I immediately felt envious. I'm not allowed to have any holes in my ears, and this girl got to have three.

Claudia Kishi wanted three, also, but I didn't feel very sorry for her, since she already had two. Claudia is one of my friends in the Baby-sitters Club. What's the Baby-sitters Club? It's a business that my friends and I run. We baby-sit for people in Stoneybrook, Connecticut, where we live.

There are six of us in the club. The president is Kristy Thomas. She was the one who started the club. She started it last year with a bunch of her friends who are all thirteen now and in eighth grade. My best friend, Jessi Ramsey, and I are the two younger members of the club. (We're both eleven and in sixth grade.) What an interesting group we are. We're very different, but we get along really well.

Kristy, for instance, is loud and outgoing. And full of ideas. She's quite serious about running the club. She's small for her age and cares zero about her appearance. In fact, she almost always wears jeans, sneakers, a turtleneck, and a sweater. She comes from a family of brothers, two older ones, and a little one, David Michael. Her mom, who was divorced, recently remarried a millionaire, so now Kristy lives in a mansion across town from her old house (and across town from the rest of us). She has a new little stepsister and stepbrother, Andrew and Karen, whom she loves to pieces. Kristy would not care one bit about having her ears pierced.

Mary Anne Spier, who is our club secretary and Kristy's best friend, couldn't be more different from Kristy. She's shy and sensitive and cries at just about anything. I think she's sentimental, too, which may explain why she's the first one of us to have a steady boyfriend. His name is Logan Bruno, and he and Mary Anne are perfect for each other. Mary Anne lives in the house next door to Kristy's old one, and across the street from Claudia. She lives with her dad and her kitten, Tigger. Her mom died a long time ago, when Mary Anne was very young. Mr. Spier used to be really strict with his daughter, but he's let up a lot lately. And since that happened, Mary Anne has taken more of an interest in her appearance. She wears clothes that are sort of preppy, but at the same time cool. I bet Mr. Spier would never let Mary Anne get her ears pierced, though.

Dawn Schafer is another good friend of Mary Anne's. In fact, I think Mary Anne has *two* best friends — Dawn and Kristy. Dawn is the club treasurer. Boy, is she different from anyone else in the club. She's a real individual. Dawn moved to Connecticut last year with her mom and her younger brother, Jeff. They moved all the way from California after her parents got divorced, and they picked Stoneybrook because Mrs. Schafer grew up here, or something like that. Dawn is so Californian that it's almost sad to see her transplanted to the East Coast. She's laid-back (but very organized and responsible), adores sunshine and

7

warm weather, and even looks Californian, with incredibly long, pale blonde hair and sparkling blue eyes. Things haven't been easy for Dawn. There was the divorce, of course, and then, just recently, her brother moved back to California to live with Mr. Schafer because he hated Connecticut so much. But Dawn is not only an individual, she's a survivor. She'll get through this. Pierced ears? I don't know whether Dawn would want them. I'm sure she'd be allowed to have them, but she'd probably only get them if she were sure she wasn't going to look like every other thirteen-year-old around.

Now, let me get back to Claudia Kishi. She's the one who already has pierced ears, remember? Claud is the vice-president of the Baby-sitters Club and probably the trendiest, coolest kid in all of Stoneybrook Middle School. She's into art and makes some of her own clothes and jewelry — wild things, like socks on which she paints palm trees and coconuts; or gigantic, bright *papier-mâché* pins and bracelets. Whether she makes her clothes or buys them, they are totally cool, and you can count on Claudia to add her own personal touches. No matter what she wears, she looks great. That's because she's Japanese-American — beautiful and exotic with dark, almond-shaped eyes; long black hair that she styles in all different ways; and an absolutely clear complexion. It's unfortunate that Claud is a poor student, because her older sister, Janine, is a genius. Claudia's parents give her grief about this, but Mimi, her grandmother, never does. Mimi is just sweet and loving.

There are just two other members of the Baby-sitters Club: Jessi and me. Since we're young, we're called junior officers. Of all the kids in the club, I guess Jessi and I are most alike, except for some obvious differences that don't matter at all. For instance, I'm white and Jessi is black. And I have seven brothers and sisters, while Jessi has just one younger sister (Becca) and a baby brother (John Philip Ramsey, Jr., nicknamed Squirt). Beyond that, well, we're both the oldest in our families but think our parents treat us like babies. We both want pierced ears desperately but will probably get braces on our teeth instead, and we both wish we could wear trendier clothes and get decent haircuts. We love to read, too, especially horse stories — although I want to be a writer one day, while Jessi dreams of maybe being a ballet dancer. (She takes lessons and is very talented.) Most important, not long ago, we were both in need of a best friend, so we were very happy to find each other after the Ramseys moved to Stoneybrook.

Claire, Margo, and I stood watching the ear-piercing. I imagined Jessi and me sitting on the stools one day. (When, though? When we were seventy-two?)

A woman with one of those ear-piercing guns approached the girl on the stool. "One more in the right lobe, is that it?" she asked.

"Yes," said the girl.

Punch went the gun.

"Aughhh!" shrieked Claire.

The woman with the gun jumped a mile. The girl on the stool looked scared to death. And Margo said weakly, "I think I'm going to barf. She just got a *hole* punched in her *ear*."

"You are not going to barf. You are *not!*" I said firmly.

I grabbed my sisters by their hands, turned them around, and ran off, calling "Sorry!" over my shoulder to the woman and the girl.

I was *so* embarrassed. Little sisters. What pains they can be.

I'll be surprised if I live to see twelve.

CHAPTER 2

"Mallory! Hey, Mal!" Jessi Ramsey was running up the sidewalk to Claudia Kishi's house.

I'd been about to go inside for our meeting of the Baby-sitters Club, but now I stopped and waited for Jessi.

"Hi," I greeted her. I could tell she'd come straight from a ballet lesson. She was still wearing her leotard — she'd just thrown a shirt and jeans over it — and her hair was pulled back from her face the way it has to be during a dance class.

"Hi," Jessi replied breathlessly.

I opened the door to Claud's house and we went inside. Us club members spend an awful lot of time at the Kishis', since club meetings are held every Monday, Wednesday, and Friday afternoon from five-thirty until six, so we hardly ever bother to ring the doorbell.

11

"Hello, girls," said a soft voice.

Mimi, Claudia's grandmother, had entered the front hallway.

"Are we the last to arrive?" Jessi asked anxiously. Jessi has such a busy schedule (between ballet lessons and a regular, twice-weekly sitting job) that she's almost always the last to show up at the meetings. This makes her a little nervous, and I understand why. She and I are not only the youngest club members, but the newest, so we feel we have to be on our toes at all times.

"Yes, you are last ones," Mimi told us, "but not late. Not five-thirty yet." (Mimi had a stroke last summer, and it has affected her speech.)

"Thanks, Mimi!" I said.

Jessi and I raced upstairs, with Mimi calling after us, "You will find surprise in Claudia room."

Surprise? I hoped it wasn't Janine, Claudia's sister. She makes me crazy.

Jessi and I ran into Claud's bedroom and stopped short. We saw the surprise right away. It was Logan Bruno, Mary Anne's boyfriend. I don't think I mentioned earlier that Logan is a member of the Baby-sitters Club. He doesn't usually come to meetings, though, since he's just an associate member, someone our club can call on to take a sitting job if none of the rest of us is free to take it.

I guess now would be a good time to stop and tell you how our club works, and I better go all the way back to the very beginning, when Kristy first got the idea for the club. That was over a year ago, before Kristy's mom was even thinking about marrying Watson Brewer, the millionaire.

What happened was this. Mrs. Thomas needed a sitter for David Michael, who was six at the time, but Kristy and her older brothers, Sam and Charlie, were all busy. So Mrs. Thomas got on the phone. Kristy watched her make call after call in search of a sitter, and while she watched, she thought what a waste of time this was for her mother. If only her mom could make one call and reach a bunch of sitters at once, she would find one much more quickly. That was when Kristy got the idea for the Baby-sitters Club. She and a few of her friends, she thought, could meet several times a week, and people could call them during the meetings and practically be guaranteed a sitter. One of the girls was bound to be free.

So Kristy got together with Mary Anne and

Claudia and a new friend of Claudia's, Stacey McGill. (I'll get back to Stacey later.) They made up fliers and began advertising their club, letting people know their meeting times and how to get in touch with them. They were in business!

The girls voted Kristy president of the Baby-sitters Club since it had been her idea, and since she's good at running things.

They made Claudia the vice-president. This is because Claudia has her own phone and personal, private phone number, so the meetings would always be held in her room. And she would probably get calls at nonmeeting times that she'd have to handle on her own.

Mary Anne was named the secretary, and she has a big job. She's neat and organized (and has nice handwriting), so the girls thought she would be good at keeping the club record book in order. The record book is where we write down our clients' phone numbers and addresses, keep track of the money we've earned (actually, that's the job of the treasurer), and most important, schedule our sitting jobs. Mary Anne has never once made a scheduling mistake.

Stacey McGill was the club's first treasurer. She kept track of the money earned and was also in charge of the club treasury. Each week, we pay dues into the treasury, and we use the money for two things: an occasional club party or sleepover, and supplies. The supplies are usually items for our Kid-Kits. Kid-Kits are another of Kristy's great ideas. Each of us has one. They're boxes we decorated and keep filled with our old games, toys, and books, as well as new things such as crayons or activity books or coloring books. Sometimes we bring them with us when we baby-sit. Kids really love them. And when the kids are happy, their parents are happy . . . and when parents are happy, they call us with more baby-sitting jobs!

Anyway, back to Stacey, the treasurer. Not long ago, Stacey had to move to New York City. Meanwhile, Dawn Schafer had arrived in Stoneybrook and joined the club. She'd been made an alternate officer, meaning she could take over the duties of anyone who might have to miss a meeting. When Stacey left, though, Dawn became the new treasurer. And then, because the club was so busy, the girls asked Jessi and me to join. They really needed help. We were named junior officers since we're only allowed to sit after school or on weekends (unless we're sitting at our own houses).

So who is Logan Bruno? Well, he and a friend of Kristy's, Shannon Kilbourne, are associate club members. As I said before, they don't come to meetings (usually). They're people we can call on in a real pinch — when none of the rest of us is free to take a job. Surprisingly, that does happen from time to time, and we hate to tell a parent that no one's available. So our associate members are very important.

And that's about it. The club is successful and fun, and Jessi and I are really glad we became members.

"Hi, you guys!" Mary Anne greeted us as we ran into Claud's bedroom. "Look who came to the meeting!"

Logan Bruno grinned at Jessi and me from his spot on the floor. I'm not very interested in boys yet, but I must admit that as they go, Logan is pretty cute. And he has this interesting southern accent. (He's from Louisville, Kentucky.)

"Hi," Jessi and I said shyly. We hadn't expected to see a boy. I was glad we looked halfway decent — and that we hadn't been running down the hall talking about underwear or deodorant or something.

"Okay, order! Order!" called Kristy. Kristy

conducts our club meetings in a businesslike way. She sits in Claud's director's chair wearing a visor, with a pencil stuck over her ear. "Any club business?" she asked as Jessi and I sat down on the floor — but not *too* near Logan.

"I have to collect dues," Dawn announced. She was sprawled on Claud's bed between Mary Anne and Claudia.

Us club members groaned but began searching our pockets or purses for money. (Logan didn't have to pay.) When Dawn had collected everything and stashed it safely in the treasury envelope, Kristy said, "Have you been keeping up with the club notebook?"

Uh-oh. I guess I forgot to tell about the notebook. It was *another* of Kristy's ideas, not to be confused with the record book. In the notebook, each of us club members is responsible for writing up every single job we go on. Then we're supposed to read the notebook once a week or so, just to keep track of what's going on with the families we sit for. It's pretty helpful — we write about sitting problems and how we solve them. That kind of thing. I like writing in the notebook, but most of the girls think it's a boring chore.

In answer to Kristy's question, the rest of us (except Logan) chorused, "Yes." She asks us about the notebook every Monday, and every Monday we tell her we've been reading it.

Club business was out of the way and we waited for the phone to ring. Sometimes we start gossiping about friends and school stuff while we wait, but with Logan there, I could tell that all of us, even Mary Anne and Logan, were a little uncomfortable.

Claudia took care of that by searching her desk drawers for a bag of pretzels she knew she'd hidden there. Claud is addicted to junk food and hides it all over her room. She has to hide it, since her parents don't approve of her bad habit. The rest of us like Claud's bad habit, though (well, Dawn refuses to eat things with sugar in them), and we eagerly dove into the bag. Wouldn't you know, as soon as our mouths were full — the phone rang.

We looked at each other in horror.

Logan, being a boy, swallowed his mouthful pretty quickly, and said, "I'll get it!"

But Kristy waved her arms at him. "No! No! Mmphh, mmphh, mmphh." After a moment, she swallowed, too, took a deep breath, and managed to say, "No. Our clients aren't used to a boy answering the phone. Not that there's anything wrong with it," she added quickly. "I just don't want to take someone by surprise."

The phone was on its fourth ring by then, so Kristy grabbed it. "Hello, Baby-sitters Club. . . . Yes? . . . Mrs. Arnold? . . . Oh, okay, I see. I'll get right back to you. 'Bye."

Kristy hung up and we all began laughing. We couldn't believe what had just happened. When we calmed down, Kristy said, "All right. That was Mrs. Arnold. You know, the mother of the twins?"

"The twins?" I repeated.

"Oh, I guess you haven't sat for them," said Kristy. "Actually, the club has only sat for them a couple of times. The Arnolds have twin daughters. They're seven. Marilyn and Carolyn — "

"Marilyn and Carolyn?!" exclaimed Logan.

"Don't tell me — they're identical," I guessed.

"Right down to the buckles on their shoes," agreed Kristy. "They're nice enough, though. I mean, they can't help how their mother dresses them — or what their names are. Anyway, Mrs. Arnold needs a steady sitter, someone who can take care of the twins two afternoons a week for the next couple of months."

"Wow," Logan said, and whistled through his teeth.

"Yeah. There's some sort of fund-raising project at Stoneybrook Elementary," Kristy went on. "That's where the twins go to school.

And Mrs. Arnold agreed to head it up. So she's going to be pretty busy, but only for the next eight weeks. She wants someone every Tuesday and Thursday afternoon from three-thirty till six. Mary Anne?"

Our secretary was already studying the appointment pages in the record book. "Boy," she said. "This is a tough one. Jessi, you're out, obviously."

"I better be out, too," said Claud. "There's a chance my art classes are going to switch to Thursdays."

"Okay," Mary Anne replied. "And Kristy, you've got several sitting jobs already lined up for Tuesdays and Thursdays. Hmmm."

After a lot of planning and discussion, I wound up with the job at the Arnolds'! I couldn't believe it. What luck! Sitting for twins would be fun. Plus, I'd be rich. I thought of all the earrings I would have been able to buy — if I'd had pierced ears.

I checked out Claud's ears. Hanging from them were little pairs of red sneakers. Cool! No one else was wearing earrings except Dawn. I could tell hers were clip-ons. They were big turquoise triangles. They were cool, too, I guess, but there was nothing like pierced ears. If only I could convince Mom and Dad. . . . And if only I could convince them to let me have my long, curly hair cut and styled. It looked like a rat's nest.

Oh, well. First things first. First I had to earn enough money for ear-piercing and hair-cutting. And in order to do that, I had to get started at the Arnolds'. I couldn't wait to begin.

CHAPTER 3

D*ing-dong.*

I stood nervously on the Arnolds' front stoop. A sitting job with a new client always reminds me of the first day of school. You have a vague idea what you're getting into, but you don't know the specifics. For instance, you know a little about who the kids are, you know you'll be responsible for them, but how will you get along with them? Will the kids like you? Will you like them? Will the kids be fun or will they misbehave? What will the parents be like?

I'd find out soon enough. I'd rung the bell, and now I could hear feet running toward the door.

I clutched my Kid-Kit and waited.

The door opened slowly and two faces peeked around it. The faces were so alike that it was as if I were seeing just one face and its reflection in a mirror.

"Hi," I said.

"Hi," replied two voices. They sounded uncertain.

The door opened the rest of the way, and before me stood Marilyn and Carolyn Arnold. Both girls were wearing blue kilts with straps that went over their shoulders, white blouses with lace edging the collars and sleeves, white knee socks, and black patent leather Mary Jane shoes. Their brown hair was cut in a bowl shape, framing their faces, and each twin had put on a blue headband with a blue bow on the side of it. Also, each wore a silver ring on the pinky finger of her right hand, and a beaded identification bracelet on her left wrist. The bracelets were the only difference between the twins. The beads on one bracelet spelled MARILYN. The beads on the other one spelled CAROLYN. I was glad I was wearing my glasses.

What a relief, I thought. As long as the girls wore their bracelets, I'd know who was who. I hoped they wouldn't take them off.

The girls were just looking at me, so I said, "I'm Mallory Pike, your baby-sitter. Can I come in?"

Marilyn and Carolyn stepped back and opened the door wider. I entered the Arnolds' house, still clutching my Kid-Kit.

"What's that?" asked one of the twins, pointing to the box.

I glanced at her bracelet. "It's a Kid-Kit, Carolyn," I replied.

Carolyn's face lit up. Why? Oh, she must have known about Kid-Kits from when other members of the Baby-sitters Club had sat at the Arnolds'.

"Do you like Kid-Kits?" I asked her. "This one has some good things in it. New coloring books and new sticker books."

"Oh, boy!" The twins jumped up and down excitedly.

"Mallory? Is that you?" called a voice from upstairs.

"Yes. Mrs. Arnold?"

"I'll be right there."

In a moment a fussy-looking woman came down the stairs. Do you know what I mean by fussy? I mean, everything about her was too much and too cute. She was wearing two necklaces, a pin, bracelets on each wrist, rings, earrings, and even an ankle bracelet. Her stockings were lacey, and she was, well, as Claud might have said, overly accessorized. Practically everything she wore had a bow attached. There were bows on her shoes, a bow on her belt, a bow in her hair, and a bow at the neck of her blouse. Her sweater was beaded, and she hadn't forgotten to pin a fake rose to it. Whew! As for cute, her earrings were in the shape of ladybugs, one of her necklaces spelled her name — Linda — in gold script, her pin was in the shape of a mouse, and the bow in her hair was a ribbon with a print of tiny ducks all over it.

"Hi, Mallory, I'm Mrs. Arnold," said the twins' mother as she reached the bottom of the stairs. She held out her hand, and we shook in a businesslike way. "I'm sure you and the girls will get along fine. They'll show you where their toys are — "

"Mallory brought toys for *us!*" exclaimed one twin.

"Why, that's lovely. Well, good. I can see that the three of you are off to a happy start."

(Blechh.)

Mrs. Arnold showed me where the emergency phone numbers were posted, made sure I knew how to reach her at Stoneybrook Elementary, gave me a few quick instructions, reminded Marilyn to practice the piano for half an hour, and then kissed each of the twins. "Good-bye, loves," she said. "I'll see you in two and a half hours — at six-o'clock."

" 'Bye, Mommy!" chorused the girls.

Mrs. Arnold left in a fog of perfume. (That was another thing. She was wearing perfume, makeup, and nail polish. She'd probably painted her toenails, too.)

"Can we see what's in the Kid-Kit?" asked one of the twins as Mrs. Arnold started her car in the garage.

(A quick glance at the bracelet.) "Sure, Marilyn," I replied, and Marilyn beamed. The twins must really love Kid-Kits. I'd have to remember to bring mine with me each time I sat.

"Let's go to our room!" exclaimed . . . Carolyn. (Bracelet check.)

Well, I'd been prepared for identical twins and identical clothes, but not for two identical halves of a bedroom. That was how the girls' room looked, though. Again, it was as if someone had placed a huge mirror in the center of the room, and it was reflecting one side. On each side were beds covered with pink flowered spreads over white pleated dust ruffles. There were matching pillows. There were twin dressers, desks, and bookshelves. There were even two white rockers. Everything was arranged symmetrically. But what was most surprising were the toys — two of everything. Two identical stuffed bears, two Cabbage Patch dolls, two, two, two.

This was almost like a science fiction movie —

but I didn't say anything. Instead, I plopped myself down on the rug and opened the Kid-Kit.

"Okay, here you go," I said. "What do you guys like? I've got books to read and puzzles and jacks and those new coloring and sticker books."

"I like to read," said one twin. (Oh, it was Marilyn.)

"I like puzzles," said Carolyn.

I handed Carolyn a small jigsaw puzzle, and she immediately dumped it on the floor. Then I pulled out a handful of books.

"Let's see, Marilyn. Here's *Baby Island*. And here's *Charlie and the Great Glass Elevator*. Oh, here are three of the Paddington books."

"Paddington!" exclaimed both twins.

"We love him!" said Carolyn. She abandoned her puzzle and leaned over to look at *Paddington Abroad*, *Paddington Helps Out*, and *Paddington Marches On*.

In a flash, Carolyn had chosen *Paddington Marches On*, Marilyn had chosen *Paddington Abroad*, and each twin was lying on her bed with her legs crossed, reading happily.

"You guys are so cute!" I couldn't help exclaiming. "Look at you. I wish I had my camera. You look like bookends."

The twins exchanged a troubled glance.

"Boggle," Marilyn whispered across the room to Carolyn. (Or did Carolyn whisper to Marilyn? I couldn't read their bracelets.)

Carolyn nodded. Then the twins went back to their books.

But not for long.

"Oom-bah," said Carolyn a few minutes later, and the girls tossed the books aside and got to their feet.

With another sidelong glance at each other, they did the last thing I'd expected them to do. Very slowly, they removed their bracelets. They tossed them onto their beds. Then they ran around the room, jumping back and forth, darting from side to side.

"Hey, you guys!" I cried. "What are you doing?"

"Chad. Pom dover glop," said one.

"Huh?"

"*Now* tell us apart," said Marilyn-or-Carolyn.

"I can't," I replied helplessly. "You don't have your bracelets on."

"Do you like to baby-sit?"

"Sure."

"Well, you won't like to sit for *us*."

(What had gone wrong?)

The girls were still moving around. Since even their voices sounded alike, I couldn't tell who was talking. For all I knew, it was just one of them, and the other was keeping quiet.

Suddenly they ran downstairs.

I chased after them. When I reached the living room, I found only one twin.

"Okay, which one are you?" I asked.

Marilyn-or-Carolyn shrugged.

"You're not going to talk?"

Another shrug. Then, without warning, she stood up and darted out of the room. I ran after her, but not quite as fast (the twins are *quick!*) and found one of them at the kitchen table.

"Which one are *you*?" I asked.

"The same as before," was the cross reply.

I felt like saying, "Well, ex*cuse me!*" But instead I said, "Where's your sister?"

Shrug.

And then an idea came to me. I don't know where it came *from*, but it seemed like a good one. I took Marilyn-or-Carolyn by the hand, hauled her into the living room, sat her at the piano, and said, "Practice time."

Marilyn-or-Carolyn looked at me helplessly.

"Go ahead. Play," I urged her. "You *can* play, can't you?"

The twin scowled. "No," she said sullenly.

"Okay, Carolyn. Thank you very much. Now

please go find your sister and tell her it's time to practice."

So Carolyn did just that, and Marilyn began her playing. For exactly half an hour, I knew which twin was which. But when Marilyn stopped practicing, I was in trouble again.

I couldn't *wait* for Mrs. Arnold to come home.

Easy money, huh, Jessi?

Definitely, Mal.

This afternoon Jessi and I sat for my brothers and sisters and we hardly had to do a thing. Everyone was busy and as good as gold.

I think we were lucky. You know how awful rainy days can be, when everyone wants to go outside.

Yeah, we were lucky. The kids entertained themselves inside.

We had time on our hands.

I know. But think of all the times my brothers and sisters have been real stinkers.

I'd rather not. I'd rather just think about the good time we had today....

31

Well, it sure was an easy sitting job. It was Sunday afternoon, and my parents had been invited to a reception. The reception was to be held indoors, which was lucky since it was pouring rain. And I mean, cats and dogs, streaming down the windows, rattling the gutters. That kind of rain. As Jessi pointed out in the club notebook, rainy days like this one can be a baby-sitting disaster if the only thing the kids want to do is go outside.

But — for once — every one of my brothers and sisters was busy and happy. The triplets were down in the rec room watching a movie that we'd rented for the weekend. Our entire family had watched it the night before, and now the triplets were watching it again. Personally, I don't see how they can do that. I can read a book over and over again, but there aren't too many movies I could watch twice in one weekend.

Nicky was upstairs in the room he shares with the triplets, working on a science-fair project. He was creating a solar system, and it wasn't easy. He had to find balls of various sizes to represent the planets, and then he had to figure out how to get them to revolve around the sun (a yellow tennis ball). It would keep him busy for hours.

Vanessa was in the bedroom she shares with me, writing poems. She keeps a fat notebook full of her poetry, and she said the rainy weather had inspired her, so she would be busy for hours, too. When Vanessa gets on a roll, she can write eight or ten long poems.

Finally Margo and Claire were upstairs in *their* room. They were playing Candy Land. Ordinarily, that causes endless arguments, and even a few tears, but they were also quiet.

"We're playing the best out of seven games," Margo informed Jessi and me when we stuck our heads in their room to make sure they were still alive.

The best of seven. That could take all day.

Jessi and I settled ourselves in the kitchen with cups of hot chocolate. (There is just nothing like hot chocolate on a rainy day, summer or winter.)

"Do you think we should split up?" Jessi asked me. "I'll sit upstairs, you sit downstairs — in case an argument breaks out or something. This seems too easy."

I smiled. "I really think everyone is okay. At the first sign of trouble, we'll separate. Right now, let's leave the kids alone and just relax."

Jessi didn't have a problem with that! We finished our hot chocolate, went into the living room, and sprawled on the rug.

33

"What would you do if you had a milllion dollars?" Jessi asked me.

"Get my ears pierced," I replied.

Jessi giggled. "Okay, after that, you'd still probably have, oh, about nine hundred thousand nine hundred and ninety bucks left. Then what would you do?"

"Get contacts. And get my hair cut and styled."

"And after *that?*"

"Pay the orthodonist *not* to give me braces."

Jessi couldn't stop laughing. "Then what?" she managed to say.

"Buy a nine-bedroom house for my family."

"So each of you kids could have your own room?"

"Exactly."

"Hmm. You'd really want separate rooms?"

"After sharing all our lives? Of course."

"Even the triplets?"

"Definitely. I mean, they spend a lot of time together, but they *are* different people. They have different interests and stuff. And sometimes they do get on each other's nerves."

"You know, it's funny. I've never had a bit of trouble telling the triplets apart," said Jessi. "Well, maybe a little when I first met them. But after that, never."

"Most people don't have any trouble," I

said. "Okay. What would *you* do with a million bucks?"

"Get my ears pierced," replied Jessi, and we both began laughing again.

"You know," I said, "I feel like a baby because Mom and Dad won't let me get my ears pierced or my hair cut or wear cool clothes. But when I think about it, maybe *they're* the babies. I mean, ear-piercing is safe if you have it done professionally. It isn't safe to have a friend do it with a needle and an ice cube, but — "

"Oh, EW! That is so disgusting! A needle and an ice cube!" cried Jessi. Then she calmed down. "But," she went on, "I don't think your parents — or mine — are babies. I know what you mean, but they must have good reasons for what they will and won't let us do."

"Whose side are you on?" I demanded, but I wasn't really angry.

Jessi smiled. "I'm just being diploma — Hey, look! Twins!"

I turned and saw Claire and Margo coming down the stairs hand in hand. Each was wearing a pair of pink sweat pants, a white turtleneck, and running shoes, with a pink bow in her hair.

"What happened to Candy Land?" I asked the girls.

35

"We got tired of it," Claire replied.

"*Claire* got tired of it," said Margo pointedly.

"Silly-billy-goo-goo," Claire said, and giggled. She's going through that five-year-old silly stage.

"So we decided to have a fashion show," Margo went on. "This is the first fashion of the year. It's the Terrific Twin outfit."

"Stunning," said Jessi.

"Superb," I added.

Claire turned around gracefully. Margo spun around and fell down.

Then they ran back upstairs.

"Gotta change," Claire yelled over her shoulder.

"New outfits coming up!" called Margo.

When they were out of earshot, Jessi said, "Remember how much fun it used to be to pretend you had a twin?"

"I guess," I answered slowly, trying to remember.

"Oh, Becca and I used to do it all the time. Once, we were wearing matching dresses and Mom took us shopping and we told everyone we were *really twins*. The only problem was, Becca and I are three years apart, and I've always been tall for my age, so I was, like, at least a whole head taller than Becca was. People must have thought we were crazy!"

I laughed. "I know Kristy and Karen" (Karen is Kristy's stepsister) "have a matching sister outfit that they get a kick out of wearing together. But I really don't remember ever pretending *I* was a twin. I do remember once, though, when our family was on vacation and Vanessa and I tried to convince people we were French. We said *oui* and *non* and spoke with an accent."

"Okay! Here we come again!" called Margo. "We're the fashion beauties. Close your eyes. When you open them, you'll see another new fashion."

Jessi and I obediently closed our eyes.

"What fashion will we be seeing?" asked Jessi while we waited.

We could hear whispering.

"You will be seeing Beach Fashion," replied Margo. "Now open your eyes."

We opened them. It was all we could do to keep from laughing. My sisters were wearing bathing suits, knee socks, some old high-heeled shoes of Mom's, and a ton of jewelry.

"Impressive," said Jessi.

"Smashing," I added.

The fashion show continued until Claire got tired of it and said, "Margo, let's play Candy Land, okay? Best out of seven."

The girls disappeared. Jessi and I made a

quick check on the rest of my brothers and sisters. Vanessa was murmuring to herself and writing in her notebook. Nicky was patiently revolving a Ping-Pong ball around the yellow tennis ball. The triplets were rewinding the movie, getting set to watch it one final time.

"All quiet on the western front," Jessi said to me as we returned to the living room.

I laughed. Jessi and I had both tried to read that book and had hated it, even though it was a classic and we knew we were supposed to like it.

"You know," I said suddenly, "I am so glad you moved to Stoneybrook. I think we make awfully good best friends."

"Definitely," agreed Jessi.

"But you know what would make my life perfect?" I asked.

"What?"

"Getting my ears pierced and looking more grown-up. Or at the very least, more human."

"Dream on," replied Jessi.

CHAPTER 5

Thursday

What pains! What rotten pains! Boy, you guys, we've had some tough baby-sitting charges before -- Jackie Rodowsky, the walking disaster; Betsy Sobak, the great practical joker; even my own brothers and sisters -- but these terrible twins are just the worst! If you have any idea how to handle them, please tell me, because I'm going crazy. No kidding.

Want to know what happened today? (Dumb question. This is the club notebook. I have to tell you what happened.) Okay, here goes. I'll start at the beginning, of course. Get prepared not to believe what you read, because I guarantee you won't. But I swear that every word is the truth.

Okay. I show up on the Arnolds' doorstep right on time, ready to start over again with the twins. I've remembered to bring the Kid-Kit....

39

Ding-dong!

I rang the Arnolds' bell, expecting to hear feet running toward the door.

Nothing.

After a moment, I rang the bell again.

"Marilyn? Carolyn?" I could hear Mrs. Arnold call. Silence. At last the door was flung open. "Hello, Mallory," said the twins' mother.

"Hi," I replied.

"Goodness, I don't know where the girls have gotten to. I'm sure they're here somewhere. I thought they would answer the door."

I stepped inside. Mrs. Arnold was patting the bow in her hair. I noticed that she was wearing three rings on that one hand — and nail polish, of course.

"Marilyn! Carolyn!" called Mrs. Arnold again. Then, "MARILYN! CAROLYN! I am going to count to three. If you're not here by then, you will be in big trouble. . . . One, two," (no twins yet) "two and a half, two and three quarters, I hope you like your bedroom because you'll be spending a lot of time there if — "

"Here we are! Here we are!"

Marilyn and Carolyn raced into the hallway. Inwardly, I sighed. They were dressed identically again. I guess I'd been hoping for . . . I don't know. But there they were — matching plaid dresses, white tights, black patent leather Mary Jane shoes, red ribbons in their hair, gold lockets, gold rings, pink nail polish, and (thank goodness) their name bracelets.

Mrs. Arnold took one look at her daughters and exclaimed, "Why, you switched bracelets again, you monkeys!" (How could she tell?) "Now switch them back. I hope you won't be teasing Mallory today."

Believe me, I hoped they wouldn't be teasing Mallory today, either.

The twins exchanged a disgusted look as they switched their bracelets, and I frantically checked them over for some sort of difference. Anything at all. A hole in somebody's tights, a chip in somebody's nail polish. Just something that would tell me which one was Marilyn and which one was Carolyn. But I could not find one difference.

"Well, good-bye, you monkeys," said Mrs. Arnold, adding a hat to her outfit. "I'll be back before you know it. Remember to practice for half an hour, Marilyn."

Mrs. Arnold left.

I stood anxiously in front of the twins. They stared at me. I held out the Kid-Kit as if it were both a shield and a peace offering.

"Kid-Kit?" I said. "You never did read those Paddington books. And I added some new puzzles, Carolyn."

"Go-blit?" said . . . Marilyn.

"Der. Blum snider,"was Carolyn's response.

And with that, the bracelets were off, tossed carelessly onto a couch in the living room.

Oh, no, I thought. But all I said was, "The least you two could do is speak English."

"Okay," replied one twin. "Let's play hide-and-seek."

"Well . . . all right." How bad could hide-and-seek be?

"We'll hide, you seek!" cried the other twin. "Stand in the hallway, cover your eyes, and count to one hundred."

"Okay." I covered my eyes and listened to the twins run off.

As they went, I thought I heard one whisper to the other, "In-bro duggan, tosh?"

"Tosh," was the answer.

I began to count. I counted out loud. I had learned to do that long ago, playing hide-and-seek with my brothers and sisters, who would accuse me of cheating and skipping numbers if I counted silently and then came looking for them before they'd found a hiding place. ". . . Twenty-three, twenty-four," I continued. (I *hate* counting to a hundred.) ". . . Ninety-seven, ninety-eight, ninety-nine, one hundred! Ready or not, here I come!"

The Arnolds' house was quiet, and I wondered if the girls were hiding outdoors. We should have made some hiding rules before we began the game. Oh, well. Too late now. Besides, I hadn't heard any doors open or close.

I began to search the house. I felt funny, as if I were invading the Arnolds' privacy, so I stuck to the kitchen and living room and dining room at first. They aren't personal, like bedrooms are.

I found one twin behind a full-length curtain in the dining room. (I could see her shoes sticking out.) "Found you!" I cried, pulling the curtain aside. "Come on and help me look for your sister."

Marilyn-or-Carolyn trailed behind me into the kitchen. "You must know all the good hiding places," I said to her. "Where should we look?"

A shrug. "I don't want to look. You're the seeker. You look. Can I have a snack? We didn't have one after school."

"Okay." Quickly I set out some juice and graham crackers. "You stay right here," I told

Marilyn-or-Carolyn. "I'll be back when I find your sister." I left the kitchen, searched the den, returned to the kitchen — and found only some graham cracker crumbs and an empty paper cup. The snack was gone and so was the twin who'd eaten it. Oh, brother.

I kept searching and came across the other twin under one of the beds in the girls' room. "Found you!" I cried.

"Can I have a snack?" asked Marilyn-or-Carolyn.

"Sure." I set her up in the kitchen with juice and graham crackers. "Now where is your sister?" I wondered.

"Isn't she hiding?"

"Yes, but I already found her once."

"Oh." Marilyn-or-Carolyn tried to hide a smile. "My sister is sneaky. I bet she hid again. She does that sometimes."

"Well, I better find her." I left the room. Of course when I returned, the snack and the twin were gone again. I should have known better.

I finally found a twin squished behind a couch in the living room, and she said, "Took you long enough. . . . Can I have a snack?"

"You've already had one," I replied.

"No, I didn't."

"Well, I gave out two snacks."

"Then you gave both of them to my sister."

"Sorry. If I knew which of you was which, that wouldn't have happened."

Marilyn-or-Carolyn scowled. Then she said, "Okay, I'm Carolyn. Now can I have a snack?"

I almost gave in, but I decided to be firm instead. Maybe that was my problem with the twins. Maybe I hadn't let them know who was boss. Besides, how could I be sure this twin was really Carolyn and she hadn't had a snack yet? I was beginning to see what the twins could do. Maybe this twin had already had two snacks and wanted a third.

"Nope. No snack," I told Marilyn-or-Carolyn. "There are two of you and I gave out two snacks. That's it. No more."

"No more? No *fair!*"

"It's very fair. Two twins, two snacks. I think you guys just fooled your*selves*."

"Gummy grog!" shouted Marilyn-or-Carolyn.

A moment later, her sister ran into the room. "What?"

"Colley-moss. Der blum tiding poffer-tot."

"Hanky? No gibble dandy."

What was going on? The girls were using their twin talk so much I didn't have a clue.

45

Well, I was sorry I made them angry. Too bad. They had tried to trick me. Oh, all right, they *had* tricked me.

For the next hour or so, Marilyn and Carolyn chattered away in their twin talk. They ignored me. But at five-thirty they couldn't ignore me. That was when I said, "Time to practice, Marilyn."

"Which one of us is Marilyn?" asked one twin.

"Oh. So you *can* speak English," I replied.

" 'Course we can. . . . Which one of us is Marilyn?"

"The one of you who hasn't practiced yet, and who has only half an hour *to* practice before her mother comes home. If she doesn't start playing the piano *now*, I'll have to tell her mother she didn't get all her practice time in."

Reluctantly, one twin sat down at the piano. While Marilyn played, I tried to talk to Carolyn, but Carolyn would have nothing to do with me. She took *Paddington Marches On* out of the Kid-Kit, opened it, and both girls ignored me again until their mother returned.

CHAPTER 6

Saturday

Well excuse me for living. but waht
is it whith these twins? Today was my
frist time babbysitting for them and mal
I see waht you mean. They are very big
pians. They triked me and they even got
me in treeoble. I have never goten in
trouble siting befor. At laest your frist
job at the arnolds started of okay. Mine
didn't even get of to a good start. It
got of to a bad start and grew worse. mal
I bet you cant' waite for mrs. arnolds
job to be over . . . .

Finally. Somebody besides me had to sit for the twins and got to see what terrors they were. I think Kristy had sat for them once quite awhile ago. And Mary Anne, too. But no one else. And no one had sat for them recently.

I was almost glad when Claudia had her bad experience with the Arnold girls. Not that I wanted her in trouble. I didn't. Not at all. It was just that, until Claud sat for the twins, I'd been worried that I wasn't a very good sitter. Like, maybe I didn't have enough control or whatever. But when I read Claud's notebook entry and saw that she'd had trouble, too, I realized the Arnold girls simply *were* trouble. They were twin trouble. Double trouble. Us baby-sitters were fine.

Anyway, Claudia took her Kid-Kit with her to the Arnolds' that Saturday morning. She'd learned, from reading my entries in the club notebook, that the twins like the Kid-Kits, so she went prepared.

Claud's job was to be longer than my afternoon jobs. She was taking care of the twins from ten in the morning until three in the afternoon while their parents went to an antique car show in Stamford. Poor Claud. Five hours with the twins. At least there were special things to keep the girls busy.

"Marilyn's piano lesson is at eleven-thirty," Mrs. Arnold told Claud. "Her carpool will arrive at eleven o'clock. She's going to be in a recital next week, and today is a special rehearsal and lesson. It'll last an hour and a half. She'll be dropped off here around one-thirty. While Marilyn's gone, Carolyn should work on her project for the science fair. Carolyn just loves science, don't you, dear?"

Claudia looked doubtfully at the twins in their red flared skirts, blue sweaters, white turtlenecks, and Mary Janes. The girls were pretty, Claud thought, and they were dressed nicely (even if they *were* a little dressed up for a Saturday morning), but somehow they had the look of terrors about them. They were scowling and didn't appear to love *any*thing, including science and piano-playing.

"Don't you love science, dear?" Mrs. Arnold repeated.

Carolyn shrugged.

"Tell Claudia what your project is called," Mrs. Arnold went on.

"The World of Electricity," replied Carolyn.

Mrs. Arnold beamed.

Claudia tried to smile back, but found it difficult. Instead, she took a look at the twins. Like I had done, she tried to find some difference between them, while they were still wearing their bracelets. (She was pretty sure they were planning to take the bracelets off as soon as their parents left.) She thought she noticed some differences in their faces, but it was hard to tell, and she didn't want the girls to think she was staring. And their clothes were impeccable. Not a scuff or a tear anywhere.

"Well, we should be on our way," said Mrs. Arnold. She showed Claud the emergency numbers and told her what she could fix for lunch after Marilyn returned from her lesson. Then she went on, "You're ready for your lesson, aren't you, Marilyn?"

Marilyn smiled sweetly. She showed her mother that her piano books were stacked on the bench in the front hallway.

"And Carolyn, you have everything you need for your project?"

"Yup."

"All right. Then we'll be off."

Mr. and Mrs. Arnold left. Before they had even backed the car down the driveway, Carolyn turned to Marilyn and said, "Snuff bat crawding fowser. Der blem, tosh?"

"Tosh," answered her sister.

Sensing what was coming, Claud said, "I guess this is the part where you guys take your bracelets off and try to confuse me, right?"

The twins hesitated, and for just a moment, Claud thought they might leave the bracelets on, just to spite her (which was what she was hoping for).

But no such luck.

"That's right!" cried Carolyn.

In a flash, the bracelets were off and twin talk was in full swing.

"You two just go ahead and play," Claud told them. "I don't care if you don't want me to be able to tell you apart." (Boy, is Claudia a cool one.) "Anyway, I'll be able to tell you apart at eleven."

"How come?" one twin couldn't help asking.

"Because at eleven, Marilyn will leave for the music school. Carolyn will be the one who stays to work on her project."

The twins looked at her. More twin talk followed.

"Well," said Claud, "I've got a good mystery to read. If you guys are just going to talk to each other, I'm going to read. You can look in the Kid-Kit, if you want."

So for the next hour, Claud read and the twins ignored her and played together. At eleven, Claud said, "Okay, Marilyn. Your ride will be here any minute. Why don't you get your books? Carolyn and I will wait outside with you."

"Okay!" One twin bounced to her feet and gathered up the piano books.

At last Claud knew which girl was which. She and Carolyn followed Marilyn outside and sat on the front stoop with her. Five minutes later, a car slowed down in front of the Arnolds'house, and the driver honked the horn.

"There's Mr. Bischoff," said Marilyn. "He's going to bring me home, too. See you later!" She ran across the lawn.

"Okay, Carolyn," said Claud to the remaining twin. "We better go inside so you can get to work on The World of Electricity." (Although what Claud knows about the world of electricity you could fit on the head of a pin.)

Carolyn went into the rec room. She opened a door and slid a display out of a closet.

"What are you going to do to your project today?" asked Claudia.

"Just fix the letters on the display and then read. I have to find out more about some experiments I could show the kids. Here are my books."

Claudia felt relieved. Not only did she know which twin was which (at least until one-thirty), but she wasn't going to have to work on The World of Electricity. She went back to her mystery while Carolyn fooled around with the display.

At eleven-thirty, the phone rang.

"I'll get it!" said Claud. She dashed into the kitchen and picked up the receiver. "Hello, Arnolds' residence."

"Yes, hello. Mrs. Arnold?"

"No, I'm afraid Mrs. Arnold can't come to the phone." (Us baby-sitters know never to say that the parents aren't home.) "This is Claudia Kishi. May I help you?"

"Well . . . perhaps. I'm Margaret Cohen. I teach piano at the music school. I've got a very tone-deaf Arnold twin here, so I'm wondering where Marilyn is."

It took Claud a moment to figure out what Ms. Cohen meant. Then she sputtered, "You mean *Carolyn's* there? The girls switched! I don't believe it!"

"Is there any way to, um, switch them back?" suggested Ms. Cohen. "I really need to work with Marilyn today."

"Well, I'm sorry. I can't bring Marilyn over. I — I can't drive yet," replied Claud. "Has Mr. Bischoff left already?"

"Yes, I'm afraid he has."

"Oh." Claudia was fuming, but she tried not to show it. "I'm sorry," she said again. "I guess Carolyn will just have to stay there until one o'clock. Do you mind keeping her?"

"Nooo. . . . But, well, I'll have to speak to

53

Mrs. Arnold about this. Will you please tell her to call me?''

"Of course,'' replied Claudia.

When she'd hung up the phone, she peeped into the rec room. Marilyn was reading a comic book. She hid it quickly when Claudia walked noisily into the room. She picked up one of the science books instead.

"You can stop pretending now, *Marilyn*,'' said Claudia.

Marilyn at least had the grace to blush and look embarrassed.

"That was Ms. Cohen on the phone. She is not pleased that you skipped this rehearsal. . . . Don't you like playing the piano, Marilyn?''

Marilyn looked surprised by the question. "I like it,'' she assured Claudia. "And Carolyn likes science. Really. We just wanted to play a trick.''

"Well, you did that, all right. I think you also got yourselves into trouble. Ms. Cohen is upset, you're missing an important rehearsal, and Carolyn is wasting time she could be spending on The World of Electricity. Now, I can't punish you,'' Claud went on. "That's not part of my job. But I can make sure I can tell you guys apart for the rest of the afternoon.''

Marilyn widened her eyes. "You can? How?''

"Like this.'' Claud took a Magic Marker out

of the Kid-Kit. Before Marilyn knew what was happening, Claud had drawn a happy face on the back of Marilyn's right hand. She knew it would wash off eventually. (Of course, when Carolyn returned later, she immediately drew a face on *her* hand, but it didn't look like Claud's, so Claud could still tell the girls apart.)

That was the only good thing about the day. When the Arnolds came home later, Claudia had to tell them about the mix-up, and they were not happy.

"I'm disappointed in both of you," said Mrs. Arnold to the twins.

"We know it must be tempting to play tricks and jokes," added Mr. Arnold, "but you have to choose the right times for them. A time when Marilyn misses a piano rehearsal is not a good time."

"And Claudia," Mrs. Arnold continued, "I must admit that I'm a bit surprised at you. We trusted you to be in charge of our daughters. We understand that it's difficult to tell them apart when their bracelets are off. Still . . . you were supposed to be responsible for them while we were out."

"I know," Claud replied, and she could feel her face burning. (This was *so* unfair!) "I'm very sorry. I'll understand if you don't want me to sit for you again. Or if you don't want anyone from our club to sit for you again, either." She hated to add that last part, but felt she had to.

"Oh, no, no," said Mrs. Arnold quickly. "Nothing like that will be necessary."

(Darn.)

Claud wondered if the Arnolds had been having trouble getting sitters lately, but of course she didn't say anything. She just offered *not* to take the Arnolds' money (they gave it to her anyway) and got out of there as fast as she could.

Malory, you can have the twines, was the last line in Claudia's notebook entry.

CHAPTER 7

Well, that was very kind of Claudia, but I didn't want the twines. They were making my life miserable. I dreaded Tuesdays and Thursdays. I dreaded them so much that sometimes I would forget, for a moment or two, about wanting pierced ears and a decent haircut. I even considered asking Kristy if I could quit the job at the Arnolds'. But I knew I couldn't do that. Couldn't ask Kristy, I mean. That would be as good as asking to be kicked out of the club. As far as I knew, no one in the club had ever backed out of a job she was signed up for just because the kids were difficult. And certainly, no one had ever been kicked out of the club.

There was something I could do, though, and that was discuss the problem of the twins with my friends at the next club meeting. I'd been writing about them in the notebook, so everyone was aware of what was going on.

Maybe Kristy or one of the other more experienced sitters would have some suggestions for me. The problem was worth bringing up.

Monday. Five-thirty. The members of the Baby-sitters Club had gathered in Claud's room. It was a typical scene.

Our president, dressed in jeans, a white turtleneck, a pink-and-blue sweater, and new running shoes, was sitting in Claudia's director's chair. Her visor was in place, and a Connecticut Bank and Trust pencil was stuck over her ear. She was looking in the record book and exclaiming over how much money we'd been earning lately.

Claudia was lying on her bed with one leg propped up on a pillow. She'd broken that leg a few months earlier and every now and then, especially if rain was on the way, her leg would give her some trouble. She looked absolutely great, though, pillow or no pillow. Her long hair was fixed in about a million braids which were pulled back and held in place behind her head with a column of puffy ponytail holders. She was wearing a T-shirt she'd painted herself, tight blue pants that ended just past her knees, push-down socks, and no shoes. From her ears dangled small baskets of fruit. She'd made those, I knew. She'd found the baskets and the fruits at a store that sells miniatures and dollhouse furniture. Claudia amazes me.

Sitting next to Claud on the bed were Mary Anne and Dawn. I might add that they were sitting fairly gingerly, like they thought that if they so much as moved, they would break Claud's leg all over again, which couldn't have been further from the truth. (Claud wasn't in *that* much pain.) Mary Anne was wearing a short plum-colored skirt over a plum-and-white-striped body suit. The legs of the body suit stopped just above her ankles, and she'd tucked the bottoms into her socks. I don't know where her shoes were. She'd taken them off. The neat thing about her outfit was that she was wearing white suspenders with her skirt. I immediately decided to use some of my hard-earned Arnold money to buy suspenders. And maybe a pair of push-down socks like Claud's. Or, if I became rich, to copy Dawn Schafer's entire outfit.

Dawn was wearing this cool oversized (*really* oversized) blue shirt. One of the coolest things about it was that it was green inside, so that when she turned the collar down and rolled the sleeves up, you could see these nice touches of green at her neck and wrists. She was wearing a green skirt — and clogs. I'd never seen a person actually wearing clogs, just photos of people in Sweden. Dawn was the only kid in school who could get away with wearing them. She is so self-possessed.

Then there were Jessi and me. We were sitting on the floor and we truly *looked* like we were in the sixth grade, as opposed to Claudia, Dawn, and Mary Anne, who might have been able to pass for high school students. Jessi and I looked dull, dull, dull. We were both wearing jeans. Jessi was wearing a T-shirt that said YOU ARE LOOKING AT PERFECTION. And she was wearing running shoes. But no interesting jewelry or anything else. Same with me. I was just wearing jeans, a plain white shirt, and running shoes. Yawn.

Kristy called the meeting to order. After we'd sworn that we'd been reading the notebook regularly, and after Dawn had collected the weekly dues, Kristy said, "Any problems? Anything to discuss?"

My hand shot up, and I didn't even wait for Kristy to nod to me. I just blurted out, "The Arnold twins are a major problem."

"I'll say," agreed Claud. She sat up and stuck some pillows behind her so she wouldn't have to be flat on her back while she tried to make her point. "That job Saturday was the pits." (Since we'd been keeping up with the notebook, we all knew what she was talking about.) "I have never been so humiliated," Claud went on. "Those girls got me in trouble. No parent has ever scolded me in front of the kids I've just sat for. The girls purposely made a big mess of things. And *why?* That's what I can't figure out."

"Me neither," I spoke up.

"No offense, Mal," added Claud, "and I *really mean* no offense, but I have to admit that I went to that job on Saturday thinking that maybe, just *maybe*, there was some sort of problem with you and the Arnolds. You know, that they were okay kids, but somehow the three of you just weren't hitting it off. In other words, that — that, um, *you* were the problem." Claud blushed.

"Don't worry about it," I said, even though I was a little hurt. "I was wondering the same thing myself. But after what happened to you on Saturday, I realized that wasn't true. The thing is," I went on, looking around at the rest of the club members, "we have problem clients. And, to quote Mom, I'm at my wit's end. I just don't know what to do about the twins."

The phone rang then, and a couple more times, too, so for awhile we were busy scheduling jobs. When we were done, Kristy said, "Mal, we've read your notebook entries, so we have a pretty good idea what's going on, but tell us again anyway. Maybe you'll think of things you didn't mention in the notebook."

"Okay," I said, and drew in a deep breath. I looked around and realized I had the complete attention of everyone in the room, which made me slightly nervous. I wanted to sound articulate. And I did *not* want to sound like a big baby, like someone who'd just run up against an annoying problem she didn't feel like handling.

"The twins," I began slowly, "*seem* like nice girls. They're always beautifully dressed, well, sometimes sort of over-dressed, but then their mother is, too. I think they're smart. Marilyn is an excellent piano player. She's been taking lessons since she was four. And Carolyn loves science. They both like to read, and I bet they do pretty well in school. Anyway, they must be smart to have invented their twin talk."

"Twin talk?" Dawn repeated.

"Yeah. You know, their private language," I explained, and Dawn nodded. "They can just babble away in it. Think how hard it is to learn a different language, like French or Spanish."

"*Tell* me about it," said Claud, rolling her eyes. She absolutely hates foreign languages, even Japanese, which Mimi sometimes tries to teach her.

"Well, if that's hard," I went on, "think how

difficult it must be to *invent* a language."

"But you know something?" said Claud, "I'm not sure the twin talk is a real language. I mean, I think Marilyn and Carolyn have made up a few secret words, but when they sit around going, 'Moobay donner slats impartu frund?' or something, I'm *positive* they just want us to *think* they have this secret twin talk. They don't understand each other any more than we understand them."

"But why?" I asked. "Why do they do that? And why do they take off their bracelets and confuse me when they're playing hide-and-seek, and try to get extra snacks and stuff? I don't get it. They're mean, and I was never mean to them."

"Maybe those are just things identical twins *do*," said Mary Anne doubtfully.

"I don't know," I replied. "The triplets are identical and they don't do stuff like that. Not even to people who can't tell them apart. And there are *three* of them. I mean, sure, they've played a few tricks, like switching places in school when there's a substitute teacher, but *all* kids try to trick substitutes. It's, like, a law."

Everyone laughed. And then the phone rang twice. Mary Anne scheduled a job for herself, and one for Kristy.

When things calmed down, Kristy said, "I

don't know that there's much you can do about the twins, Mal. It sounds like you're being the best sitter you can be, and they're just brats. You'll have to finish up your job with them, but after that, I won't expect anyone" (Kristy looked around the room at all us club members) "to feel she has to take a job at the Arnolds'. If Mrs. Arnold calls again, we'll just tell her we're busy. I don't like doing that, but I think we'll have to. Or we'll ask Logan or Shannon if one of them wants to brave twin trouble."

I nodded. "Okay. I guess you're right. But if anybody gets an idea about how to handle Marilyn and Carolyn, please tell it to me. . . . Boy, it's too bad they're so rotten. They're really cute little kids. Even their identical clothes are cute. There's just something . . . sweet . . . about seeing those lookalikes. I bet people stop them on the street to tell them how adorable they are."

"Nobody would ever stop me on the street to tell me I'm adorable," said Kristy.

"Me neither," added Jessi.

"Maybe they would stop me," I said, "if I didn't look like such a nerd."

"You don't look like a nerd," said Claud quickly.

"Thanks," I replied, "but yes I do. I wouldn't if I had pierced ears and a better haircut, though. I'd look at least twelve, not nerdy, and adorable.''

Dawn smiled. "What would you do to your hair?'' she asked me.

"I'm not sure. Cut it short, I think, so it wouldn't be such a wild tangle of curls.''

"I want pierced ears and decent hair, too,'' spoke up Jessi.

"I want one more hole in my right ear.'' (That was Claud, of course.)

"And I want to get back to business,'' said Kristy.

And just as she said that, the phone rang. Kristy gave us a look that said, "See? We *are* here to do business, you guys.''

But the caller was Stacey McGill, our former treasurer. Claud began shrieking, and begged to speak to her first. Then Dawn, Mary Anne, and even Kristy chatted with her.

Jessi and I grinned. Club meetings are great, especially when something fun like this happens. But part of me was disappointed. I hadn't gotten any suggestions on how to work with the troublesome twins — and I would have to face them again the very next afternoon.

CHAPTER 8

Tuesday

To quote Claudia, "Oh, my lord!" What a day today was. I sat for the twins again, and they were their usual pill-y selves — at first. Then something happened that changed our relationship. I wouldn't say we're best friends now, but I think we're going to get along better. You know that saying, "Fight fire with fire"? Well, that's what I did today, and the twins and I ended up talking and really having fun. (Funny, but I owe it all to my brothers, and they don't even know it.)

It started when the twins began speaking in their twin talk the second their mother left, and barely said a word to me in English. I couldn't stand it!...

Tuesday afternoon. I turned up at the Arnolds' at the regular time. Mrs. Arnold flurried out the door in a blur of jewelry, nail polish, and accessories. I heard the car door slam in the garage, and she was off.

I was sitting on the floor in the living room, the Kid-Kit opened in front of me. I was looking hopefully at the twins.

Marilyn and Carolyn, dressed in blue sailor dresses, red hair ribbons, white tights, and their Mary Janes, took off their bracelets, dangled them rudely in front of me, and dropped them on the floor.

"Good," I said. "Why should today be different from any other day? I think it would confuse me terribly if I could tell you two apart."

I don't know what kind of answer I was expecting from them. Maybe no answer. That was just something to say, something rude because the girls were rude and I was feeling cross.

"Poopah-key," said one twin in a voice as cross as mine had been.

I sighed. I deserved that. "Look," I said, rummaging around in the Kid-Kit. "Here's a sticker book. Oh, and Carolyn, I brought you a book about electricity. I borrowed it from

Adam. He's one of my brothers."

The girls remained standing.

"Do you want to look at the book?" I asked.

I was sure one of the girls was going to reply, "Which one of us is Carolyn?" Instead, the answer was, "Tibble van carmin."

That was a first. The girls usually spoke English in the beginning of the afternoon, or if I asked them a question. This was the first time they had completely ignored me. Well, they weren't *ignoring* me, but they might as well have been. They were ignoring me in twin talk.

"How about puzzles?" I asked.

"Zoo mat," replied one twin. But at least the girls sat down then.

"Chutes and Ladders?" I tried. "Dominoes?"

"Perring du summerflat, tosh?" asked one.

"Du mitter-mott," replied the other.

"Okay. Go ahead. Have fun," I said to the girls. I pulled my copy of *Dicey's Song*, by Cynthia Voigt, out of my purse, sat on the couch, and began to read. The twins pawed through the Kid-Kit, babbling to each other.

After about ten minutes, one of them stood up and said, "Mallory, can I have an ice-cream sandwich? We have a box of them in our freezer."

My first reaction was to say, "Oh, thank

goodness you're speaking English again." But I didn't jump in with that answer, which I knew the twins were expecting. Out of the blue a very different kind of answer came to me, and somehow I knew that it was exactly the right thing to try. I didn't have anything to lose, and it might be kind of fun. At any rate, I could give the twins a taste of their own medicine. Fighting fire with fire.

I answered the question in pig Latin. "At's-thay ine-fay ith-way ee-may."

Marilyn-or-Carolyn looked stunned. "What?" she said.

"Oh-gay on-hay. I-hay on't-day are-cay."

The twins glanced at each other in confusion. The other one spoke up warily. "What are you saying?" she asked.

"I'm-hay aying-say at-thay oo-yay an-cay ave-hay a-hay ack-snay. O-say an-cay our-yay ister-say."

"I can't understand you!" cried Marilyn-or-Carolyn in frustration.

I smiled. "Oo-tay ad-bay."

"But can I have an ice-cream sandwich?"

"Ure-shay. Ine-fay ith-way ee-may."

The twin stamped her foot. Was she getting ready to throw a tantrum? I decided I didn't care if she was.

"I want an ice-cream sandwich!" she cried.

"Me too!" cried her twin.

"Ood-gay. Oh-gay on-hay. Ut-whay are-hay oo-yay aiting-way or-fay?"

"Talk to us!" demanded the twin.

"I-hay am-hay alking-tay oo-tay oo-yay. Oo-yay ust-jay on't-day understand-hay ee-may." I was speaking as fast as I could, which made the pig Latin sound even odder.

"Talk in English! Talk right!" yelled the foot-stamper.

I gave in. "You two haven't been speaking to *me* in English," I pointed out.

"Malvern toppit samway," said Marilyn-or-Carolyn.

"Ut's-whay is-thay? Ore-may in-tway alk-tay?"

"Are you going to talk like that all after-noon?" asked one of the girls angrily.

"Nope," I replied. "Only as long as you and your sister talk in *your* language. When you stop, I'll stop."

"Maybe we don't want to stop," said Mari-lyn-or-Carolyn.

"Aybe-may I-hay on't-day either-hay," I answered.

"Okay, okay, okay. We'll stop."

"Good," I said. "But now you know how it feels when you leave someone out of a con-versation. Or when you're rude to her."

70

The twins scowled but didn't apologize. Finally one said, "What language were you talking in?"

"Pig Latin," I told her.

"Pig Latin?" The girls couldn't help smiling.

I nodded. "I could teach it to you. Anyone can learn it. My brothers taught it to me. They talk in it sometimes when they need a private language. Of course," I went on, "you've got a language of your own, so you probably don't need pig Latin."

"Oh, yes! Yes, we do!" cried one twin.

And that was when I decided that Claudia was probably right: twin talk wasn't much of a language at all, except for a few words the girls had made up. If it was, they wouldn't be so eager to learn pig Latin.

"I'll teach you pig Latin on two conditions," I said to the twins.

"What?" they replied. Instantly, they were on their guard.

"One, that you put your bracelets on — and on *right*. I'll just have to trust that you do it right. But I really want to be able to tell you apart. And two, that after I teach you pig Latin, you stop using your own language around me, because I don't like it. Is that a deal?"

The twins whispered to each other. Then one said, "If you ask for two things, then we want two things, too. We want to learn pig Latin, *and* we want the ice-cream sandwiches."

"Fair enough," I replied. "Put your bracelets on and follow me into the kitchen."

The girls did so. They sat at the table while I took three ice-cream sandwiches out of the freezer. Then I joined them. I passed out the sandwiches. As we were unwrapping them, I said, "Thank you for putting the bracelets back on. I appreciate that."

"Do you really want to be able to tell us apart?" asked . . . Marilyn. (Bracelet check.) "We are *so* tired of looking alike."

"Yes. I really do. There must be *some* difference between you. Something besides the bracelets."

"We-ell," said Carolyn slowly, "there is one thing."

"Are you going to *tell* her?" spoke up Marilyn, sounding worried.

Carolyn nodded. "It's all right. She said she really wants to know. . . . Okay?"

Marilyn nodded.

"Look very, very closely at our faces," said Carolyn.

"Look at our cheeks," Marilyn added.

I stared and stared. At last I saw a tiny mole on Carolyn's left cheek, under her eye. Marilyn had a mole, too, under her right eye. "The moles?" I asked.

The girls nodded. "It's the only difference between us that's really easy to see," Carolyn told me.

"Thank you," I replied. "Now I'll keep my part of the bargain and teach you pig Latin. It's really simple. All you do is take the sound at the beginning of a word, drop it, say the rest of the word, and follow it up with that sound plus 'ay.' Like, 'Marilyn' would be 'Arilyn-may'. Or 'Carolyn' would be 'Arolyn-cay.' Or 'table' would be — "

"Able-tay!" cried Marilyn.

"Right!" I said. "Good. Now here's a harder one. What would 'twin' be?"

The girls frowned. "Win-tay?" guessed Carolyn.

I shook my head. "For a word like 'twin,' you take the whole sound at the beginning of the word — not just the first letter — and move it around. So 'twin' would be 'in-tway.' "

"What if a word begins with a vowel?" asked Marilyn. "With 'a' or 'e' or 'i' or 'o' or 'u.' Then what? What would 'apple' be? 'Apple-ay'?"

"Nope. That's the only other rule you have to learn. When a word begins with a vowel, you stick an 'h' in there. 'Apple' would be 'apple-hay.' Or 'island would be 'island-hay.' "

"Oh! Cool!" exclaimed Marilyn.

"Easy!" said Carolyn.

And the rest of the afternoon was a dream. The girls didn't use any twin talk, and they didn't switch their bracelets.

Then Mrs. Arnold came home and asked me the last question I would have expected to hear.

"The twins' eighth birthday is coming up," she began. "They're going to have a big party. I was wondering if you and two of your friends would want to help at the party. You know, organize games, keep an eye on the kids. Do the girls in your club ever do that kind of thing?"

"Well, yes," I replied. "Not very often, but we have helped at parties."

I couldn't believe she would hire other club members after what had happened with Claudia. But Saturday seemed forgotten. "When will the party be?" I asked.

Mrs. Arnold told me, and I took down all the information — how long the party was supposed to last, how many kids had been invited, etc.

"I'll tell the girls about it at our club meeting

tomorrow, and then I'll call to let you know if we can do it, okay?"

Mrs. Arnold nodded. She seemed pleased.

So did the girls.

When I left, they called, "Ood-gay eye-bay!" instead of "Snod peer," which was what they had shouted the last time I'd left their house.

CHAPTER 9

Sunday

Today was pretty interesting. I thought it was going to be just another afternoon sitting job at my house, but I guess by now I should know better. There isn't any such thing as just another sitting job -- not with Karen, Andrew, and David Michael. Oh, nothing bad happened, but something surprising did. You never know what to expect from little kids. I guess the important thing to remember is that a kid is not just a kid. A kid is a person -- a human being -- who happens to be shorter and younger than an adult.

Anyway, the afternoon started off quietly. Hannie and Linny Papadakis came over to play with Karen and David Michael, while I tried to help Andrew memorize lines for this program he's going to be in at his preschool....

Kristy has said so herself: Her favorite sitting charges of all are David Michael, Andrew, and Karen. Well, I wouldn't expect anything different. After all, they're her little brother, stepbrother, and stepsister. Plus, they are awfully cute and fun. If I didn't have so many brothers and sisters of my own, Kristy's brothers and sister might be my favorite sitting charges, too.

Kristy was sitting because her two older brothers were out somewhere, and her parents had gone to another estate sale. That seems to be Mr. and Mrs. Brewer's new hobby. An estate sale is like a very, very, very fancy yard sale. At an estate sale, the contents of a whole house are being sold, so instead of walking around someone's front yard, looking at chipped plates and falling-apart couches, you walk through someone's house, looking at all their furniture and valuable stuff. The big difference between a yard sale and an estate sale is how much everything costs. At a yard sale, you could probably get a lamp for two, maybe three, dollars. At an estate sale, things are in good condition and sometimes cost an awful lot of money.

Kristy's mom and stepfather have started

going to estate sales to find interesting things for their house and yard. Once, they came back with a birdbath. Another time, they found a chandelier. And another time, they got this big lampshade, that looks like it's made of stained glass. Kristy thinks the things they find are weird. I think they're fun. At any rate, the Brewers had gone off in search of wall sconces (whatever those are), and Kristy was left in charge.

Andrew and Karen only live with their father part-time — every other weekend, every other holiday, and for two weeks each summer. The rest of the time, they live with their mom and stepfather, who are also in Stoneybrook. Believe me, Kristy really looks forward to the weekends with Karen and Andrew. She loves them to bits — which I think makes David Michael a little jealous, since he's so close to their ages. (She loves David Michael, too, of course.)

When Mr. and Mrs. Brewer had left, the three kids immediately began telling Kristy what they wanted to do that afternoon.

"I want to play with Hannie," Karen announced.

Hannie Papadakis is Karen's best friend when Karen is at her father's house. Hannie lives across the street and a couple of houses down. Her older brother, Linny, is David Michael's friend.

"And I want to play with Linny," added David Michael.

"How about you, Andrew? What do you want to do?" Kristy asked.

"Daddy said I have to work on my part for the program."

"The program?" Kristy repeated. "Oh, right. At school."

Andrew's entire preschool class was planning a program for the parents. Andrew did not want to be in it. He's terribly shy. But every kid was supposed to be involved, so Andrew had some lines to learn. He was playing a roller-skating bear (on pretend skates) in a circus skit — and he wasn't happy about it.

"Okay, Andrew," said Kristy, "I'll help you with your lines. Karen, why don't you call Hannie and Linny and invite them over?"

"Goody!" exclaimed Karen. "Thanks, Kristy."

Kristy took Andrew into the den to work on his lines. She chose the den because it's a smallish room and very cozy. She thought it might help Andrew to feel more comfortable.

Andrew stood in the middle of the room,

and Kristy sat on the couch, holding the paper that Andrew's teacher had sent home with him. On it were the lines for the skating bears skit. Andrew's lines were highlighted in yellow.

"All right," said Kristy. "Let's see. It says here that the ringmaster — "

"Jason is the ringmaster," Andrew interrupted.

"Okay, that Jason the ringmaster says, 'And now, all the way from Europe, here are the famous skating bears!' "

"Right," said Andrew. "Then I'm supposed to stand up and say, 'I am . . . I am' . . . um . . . Kristy, I forget what I'm supposed to say, and anyway I don't want to say it. I don't want to stand up and talk at *all*."

"I know you don't," Kristy replied gently, "but you have to. That's your job. You know how your daddy and mommy both have jobs and go to work?"

"Yeah."

"And my mother and your stepfather have jobs and go to work?"

"Yeah."

"Well, I have jobs, too. My jobs are baby-sitting and going to school. Going to school is also a job for Charlie, Sam, David Michael,

Karen, and you. And part of *your* job is to be in this program."

"But I don't want to be in it," replied Andrew, and his lower lip began to quiver. "I don't want everyone looking at me and listening to me."

"But you know what they'll probably be thinking while they're doing that?"

"What?"

"They'll probably be thinking, What a good bear that Andrew makes. He knows his lines so well. I bet he worked very hard."

"What if I forget my lines? Then what will they be thinking?"

"They'll be thinking, Oh, too bad. He forgot his lines. Well, that happens sometimes. He *still* looks like a very nice, smart boy."

Andrew didn't seem convinced, so Kristy only worked with him for a few minutes. Then she let him go to his room. He said he wanted to be alone.

"Karen!" Kristy called. "David Michael! Where are you guys?"

Kristy had heard the doorbell ring while she was talking to Andrew, so she assumed the Papadakises had come over. Sure enough, she found Linny and David Michael on the back patio reading Basho-Man comics. Then she went to Karen's room, where she found the girls. They were dressed as twins!

"Look!" cried Karen. "Look what Hannie got! It's a dress exactly like ours!" Karen was wearing her sister-outfit dress that Kristy's grandmother had given her and Kristy the previous Christmas.

"My mommy bought it for me," Hannie spoke up, "and as soon as I saw it, I said, 'That's just like Karen's dress.' So I wore it over as a surprise."

"And we both have on white tights," added Karen, "and our shoes almost match." The girls were wearing Mary Janes, but Hannie's had two straps each, while Karen's had just one.

"Are we twins?" asked Hannie, putting her arm around Karen.

Kristy smiled. The girls couldn't have looked less like twins. Karen is blonde-haired, blue-eyed, and thin, while Hannie is dark-haired, dark-eyed, and stocky, but Kristy said, "You look just like twins."

The girls beamed.

"Let's do something twins do!" cried Karen. "Let's . . . let's . . ."

Kristy left the girls deciding what to do. She had an idea of her own. She went to her room and found *her* matching dress. She took off her jeans and turtleneck and put the dress on.

"Whoa," she whispered. "This thing's *tight*." Kristy is the shortest kid in her grade at Stoneybrook Middle School, but she must have been growing. The thought made her happy.

She barely managed to zip up the dress. Then she found a pair of white stockings and looked for some black shoes. She didn't have Mary Janes, of course, but she found some black flats and slipped into them.

She smiled at herself in her mirror. Then she returned to Karen's room.

"Hi, you guys!" she said.

Karen and Hannie turned to look at their "triplet."

"What do you think?" asked Kristy, pleased with her idea.

"I — " Karen began. "It's — " She gave Hannie an odd look. At last she said, "I think — I think we're tired of being twins."

"Yeah," agreed Hannie.

"You are?" said Kristy.

The girls nodded. "I think I'll change," added Karen.

"Then I will, too," said Kristy.

Kristy left the girls and put her jeans on again. She checked on Andrew, whom she found muttering his skating-bear lines in his room. Kristy smiled. Andrew was afraid and shy, but if he *had* to perform, he wanted to do it well. Kristy was proud of him.

She tiptoed away from his room and ran into Karen and Hannie, who were heading downstairs. Karen was no longer wearing her twin dress.

Interesting, Kristy wrote in the club notebook. *Jessi said girls this age like to pretend they're twins, but Karen said they got tired of the game.*

I thought about that for a long time after I read Kristy's notebook entry. I thought about some of the things Marilyn and Carolyn had said to me. I thought about what Jessi had said — that it's fun to *pretend* you have a twin, someone who looks just like you.

Then I thought about me. I remembered the time a year ago when I had bought this very cool floppy bow for my hair. Vanessa liked it so much that two days later, she bought one, too. I was so angry. Whenever Vanessa wore her bow to school, I wouldn't wear mine. I wanted to be the only one with that bow. I wanted to be an individual — like Dawn. Dawn never follows the crowd. She insists on being unique, on being *herself*.

I thought of all these things, and suddenly something clicked. I had an idea about the troublesome twins. And I had an idea about how I might help them make a little change in their lives . . . or maybe a big change.

CHAPTER 10

Saturday

Wow! Some birthday party!!
So what did you think
about the twins, Dawn?

I think they're brats, Mary
Anne.

Oh, but they aren't. I've got them all figured
out.

You're prejudiced, Mal. You've
been sitting for them.

No, honest. I have figured out the trouble
with the twins. But, look, you guys, we better
start back at the beginning and describe
this sitting job. Over to you, Dawn.

Well, the beginning is that
Mallory and Mary Anne and I were
the three sitters who ended up
helping out at the Arnold twins'
birthday party....

And *I*, Mallory, think the party turned out to be fun. Well, maybe not fun exactly, because it was work, and there were some bad moments with the twins. On the other hand, any party is exciting, and there were also some good moments with the twins. The thing is, only the twins and I knew that they were good moments. . . . Hmm, like I said before, I better start at the beginning.

The birthday party was supposed to go from one o'clock to three o'clock on Saturday afternoon. Mrs. Arnold asked us sitters to work from twelve to four so we could help prepare for the party beforehand and clean up afterward.

Mary Anne and Dawn walked over to my house, picked me up, and then the three of us walked to the Arnolds'. We arrived at ten minutes to twelve, which pleased Mr. and Mrs. Arnold.

"Happy birthday, Marilyn! Happy birthday, Carolyn!" I exclaimed as soon as I saw the twins. I'd gotten pretty good at telling them apart, even without their bracelets. Once I'd learned to look for the mole, I found other differences between the girls. For instance, Marilyn's nose is just slightly more rounded than Carolyn's. And Carolyn's cheeks are fuller than Marilyn's. But those are just physical differences. As I came to know the girls better — as they *let* me know them better — I found personality differences, too. After all, they *are* two different people, not Marilyn-or-Carolyn, so they're as different as any two sisters, or even any two strangers.

"Hi, Mallory!" cried the twins. They were bouncing up and down with excitement, still in their pajamas (matching, of course). They were not going to get dressed until just before the party started.

I introduced Dawn to the girls and their parents, and then Mary Anne said hello to everyone.

After that we got down to work.

"Let's see," Mrs. Arnold said. "Dawn, you're the tallest. Why don't you help Mr. Arnold put up the crepe paper in the dining room? Mary Anne, you can help the girls blow up balloons. And Mallory, you can fill the goody bags and then give me a hand in the kitchen."

"Okay," I replied.

Mrs. Arnold showed me into the living room, where an assembly line had been set up on the floor — fifteen paper bags with clown faces on them, fifteen packages of neat-looking barrettes (apparently, all the guests were going to be girls), fifteen sets of Magic Markers, fifteen tiny clip-on koala bears, fifteen candy bars, and fifteen beaded necklaces.

Boy, goody bags had certainly improved since I last got one. When we were little, didn't goody bags just have, oh, peanuts and a pencil and maybe a plastic ring in them?

I stuffed the bags neatly and stacked them on a chair in the living room. Then I helped Mrs. Arnold set out paper plates and cups and napkins, and fill candy baskets for the table. After that, we put the finishing touches on the twins' birthday cake. I wrote HAPPY BIRTHDAY, MARILYN AND CAROLYN in pink frosting. Believe me, this was not easy. But Mrs. Arnold thought the cake looked fine.

"It's perfect," she said. "Now let me think. Mallory, could you help the girls dress, please? I've laid their clothes out on their beds."

"Sure," I replied. "Marilyn, Carolyn!" I called. "Time to get dressed."

The girls and I went upstairs.

"Your mom said she laid your clothes out," I told them on the way.

No response.

Now what? I wondered.

We entered the girls' room. There on the beds were two absolutely beautiful dresses. They were white with pink ribbon running in rows from the neck to the waistline, and with lace at the collar, the edges of the sleeves, and all around the bottom.

"Those are gorgeous!" I exclaimed as soon as I saw them. "Are they new?"

"Yes," replied Carolyn shortly.

She and Marilyn looked at each other, looked at the dresses, then looked at each other again.

I decided to take a chance. "Gosh," I said, trying to sound casual, "you guys probably don't like having to dress the same all the time. I'm not sure I'd like it."

The twins' eyes widened in surprise. Then Marilyn said slowly, almost as if she were afraid to say it, "It's funny. Last year we *loved* wearing the same dresses. This year, it just doesn't seem like fun anymore. Hardly anyone knows whether I'm Marilyn or Carolyn. No one even cares."

"It's like we're one person instead of two," Carolyn added.

A-ha!

"Maybe you could dress differently today," I suggested. "One of you could wear your sailor dress. That would be good for a birthday party."

Carolyn's face lit up at the thought, but then she said, "No. We have to wear what Mommy says."

So on went the two white dresses — and

two pairs of pink tights, two pairs of Mary Janes, two gold lockets, two pink hair ribbons, and the name bracelets.

No sooner were the girls dressed, than the doorbell rang.

"They're here!" cried Marilyn. "The kids are here!"

The twins made a dash for the front door. Standing on the stoop outside were three dressed-up little girls. Each was holding two identical presents.

"Come on in!" said Mr. Arnold heartily. And the girls stepped into the living room. They put their presents in two piles on the couch.

For the next fifteen minutes, the doorbell kept ringing and guests kept arriving. Each one came with two gifts which were placed on the two piles. When all the children had arrived and Mary Anne and Dawn were organizing them for pin-the-tail-on-the-donkey, I secretly added my own gifts to the piles. I slipped them underneath the other presents.

Marilyn and Carolyn had seemed a little upset while they were getting dressed, but they were just fine during the games. All the girls liked pin-the-tail-on-the-donkey. Marilyn and Carolyn giggled and shrieked as they and their guests wandered blindly around the rec room, groping for the donkey poster. By the time everyone had had a turn, there were tails tacked up all over the rec room. The winner was the one who had pinned the tail on the donkey's nose. The twins were hysterical.

After the prize had been awarded, the kids played musical chairs (twice, Carolyn fell on the floor), and then they had a peanut hunt. When the hunt was over, Mrs. Arnold said, "Time for presents!"

The kids began cheering. The guests were as excited as the birthday girls were.

Marilyn and Carolyn sat down on the floor in the living room and their father set one stack of gifts beside each girl. The twins reached for the presents at the very top of the stacks. They were wrapped in Winnie-the-Pooh paper and were from a pigtailed girl named Jane. Marilyn and Carolyn tore off the wrapping. In each box was a small Raggedy Ann doll.

"Thank you," the twins said at the same time, and set the dolls on the floor.

They opened the next packages — two Barbie dolls. Then two stuffed elephants, then matching necklaces. Two, two, two. Each twin kept tossing her presents onto the floor, and growing crosser-looking by the second, although the guests kept exclaiming, "Aw, isn't that cute?" or "Oh, can I play with that?"

At last, the only presents left were mine. They were not the same size or shape. They were wrapped in different paper. The twins looked intrigued.

"Is this a mistake?" asked Carolyn.

"Who are they from?" asked Marilyn.

"Me," I replied. "Go on. Open them."

So they did. I'd picked out a tiny pin in the shape of a piano for Marilyn, and a book of simple science experiments for Carolyn.

"Boy, thanks!" cried the girls enthusiastically. They absolutely beamed at me.

But their smiles didn't last long. Mrs. Arnold wanted to take some pictures. She took the twins standing together holding hands. She took them cradling their new Raggedy Anns with the party guests grouped behind them. She took them sitting next to their piles of identical gifts. The girls were always together, always doing the same things.

It was no wonder that by cake time, the twins' faces were identical thunderclouds. They were sitting at one end of the decorated dining room table, the cake between them.

"Now lean over and blow out the candles," instructed Mrs. Arnold, her camera poised.

Two angry faces blew out the candles, then turned toward the camera.

Click!

The camera caught me in the background. I was trying to smile, but I'll bet my face looked pretty strange. I felt terrible for the twins. How awful to have no identity, to be just Marilyn-or-Carolyn, a cute lookalike twin.

As I walked home from the party later that day, I knew that my idea had been right. The girls didn't want to look identical. They might have enjoyed it when they were younger, but now they wanted to be individuals, just the way Dawn does — just the way almost everybody does — and I planned to do something about it.

CHAPTER 11

The next time I sat for Marilyn and Carolyn Arnold was on Tuesday, three days after their birthday party. The girls were waiting for me when I arrived. They were sitting side by side on the front stoop. In their matching yellow jumpsuits and white T-shirts they looked like gateposts marking the entrance to the house. When I was still only halfway up the walk, though, I noticed one difference between them. Marilyn was wearing the piano pin I'd given her.

"Hi, Mallory! Hi, Mallory!" the twins cried as I approached. They jumped up and ran to me, throwing their arms around my waist.

What a welcome.

"Hi, you guys!" I replied with a smile.

"We couldn't wait for you to get here," said Carolyn, taking one of my hands.

"You want to play with our new toys?"

asked Marilyn, taking my other hand.

The twins led me inside, where the three of us were greeted by Mrs. Arnold. As soon as she left, we went upstairs to their bedroom so I could look at their gifts. (A good project, since I'd forgotten to bring the Kid-Kit.) I'd seen the gifts the girls had received at the party, of course, but I hadn't seen the ones from their parents or relatives.

"These are from Aunt Elaine and Uncle Frank," said Carolyn, holding up two sticks. Attached to the ends of each was a long rope that fell beneath the stick in a loop.

"What are they?" I asked.

"Jump sticks," answered Carolyn. "See?" She put one of them down, held onto either end of the other, the stick poised in front of her at waist level, and made the rope circle up over her body. Jump, jump, jump. It was like a skipping rope, except that you held onto the stick instead of the ends of the rope.

"Neat!" I said. "But that looks like a better outdoor toy than an indoor one."

Carolyn obediently set the stick on the floor.

"Mommy and Daddy gave us these," spoke up Marilyn. She was pointing to two brass doll beds. Each had been placed at the foot of the girls' own beds.

"Boy," I said, "I never had anything like those." We aren't poor, but with eight kids in your family, you don't get duplicate copies of brass doll beds. You don't even get one brass doll bed.

"Now," said Carolyn, "you have to come downstairs to see our biggest presents."

Biggest presents? The doll beds weren't enough?

The twins took my hands again and led me to the rec room. There, on the floor, were two dollhouses. Pretty impressive ones, I might add.

"Look," said Marilyn. She ran to one house and pressed a button. Lights came on in each room! You should have seen those houses. They were decorated with everything from furniture (naturally) to teeny-tiny books and teeny-tiny plates of food. In each attic were a Christmas tree, a wreath, and garlands of greens, so the houses could be decorated for Christmas.

I was speechless.

But I was even more speechless after Marilyn said, "Guess what our best presents are."

"The dollhouses," I replied immediately.

"Nope," said Marilyn. "The piano pin and the science book."

"*My* presents?!" I exclaimed. "You're kidding! How come?" But already I knew the answer. I just hadn't realized how strong the girls' feelings about individuality were.

"Because . . . because," Marilyn said, giving her sister a sidelong glance, "they were different."

"And they were meant just for us, "added Carolyn. "I mean, you know, a piano for Marilyn because of her lessons, and the book for me because of the science fair."

"It seems like you know us," said Marilyn. "Is — is that silly?"

"Of course not," I answered seriously. "It isn't silly at all. Did I tell you that three of my brothers are triplets?"

"No! They are?" exclaimed Carolyn.

"Yup. And our family never treats them like they're all one person. I think maybe that's because there are so many kids in our family. There wouldn't be any point in treating three of them like one person, and the rest of us like five different people."

"So," said Marilyn, "you mean your brothers don't dress alike?"

"Nope," I said.

"Or have three of everything?"

"Nope. Unless they want three of something that isn't too expensive."

The twins looked thoughtful. "How come," Carolyn ventured after a moment, "you thought it was so neat that Marilyn and I *are* lookalikes and have all the same things?" I must have appeared sort of blank because she went on, "Remember that first day you sat for us?" I nodded. "Well, in the very beginning you tried to tell us apart, but then . . . then you were just like everyone else. You said, oh, how cute we were in our matching outfits and stuff. We decided we weren't going to be nice to any baby-sitters anymore."

So *that* had been my mistake.

"I'm sorry," I apologized. "Really I am. But you *were* cute. I didn't mean that I didn't care who you were. I just meant you were cute."

"Then we're sorry, too," said Carolyn. "We didn't understand."

"Yeah, we're sorry, too," added her sister.

I smiled. "You know, I've been thinking. Would you like to talk to your mother about how you feel? I'd help you." Please say yes, I begged silently. This was my plan and I wanted it to work.

"Talk to our mother about . . . what?" asked Marilyn.

The twins looked mystified.

I had thought it was obvious. "About *you* two. About letting you be individuals, separate people. Marilyn, if you could wear any kind of clothes you wanted, what would they look like?" I asked.

"More grown up," was her answer. "Like skirts without straps and stuff."

"Carolyn, how about you?"

"More cool," she said immediately. "Push-down socks and zipper jeans and barrettes with ribbons on them."

"You see?" I went on. "You guys like different things. It isn't just that you don't want to dress the same anymore, you also want to dress like *you*. You are two different girls and you have different tastes. Just like my sisters and I have different tastes."

"And you'd help us talk to our mother?" asked Marilyn.

I nodded. "How about it?"

"Yes!" cried the girls.

Talking to the twins' mother had seemed like a good idea when I'd first thought of it — but by the time Mrs. Arnold came home, I was a wreck. What right did I have, I wondered, butting into another family's business?

I had promised the girls I would help them talk, though, so as soon as Mrs. Arnold had paid me, I drew in a deep breath and said,

100

"Um, I was wondering. Could Marilyn and Carolyn and I talk to you?"

"Of course," replied Mrs. Arnold. "Is there a problem?" She began to look worried.

"Well, yes," I answered. "Not a baby-sitting problem, but . . ."

"Let's sit down," suggested Mrs. Arnold.

We stepped into the living room. I sat on the couch with one twin on either side of me. Mrs. Arnold sat across from us in an armchair.

I cleared my throat. I wasn't sure where to begin. At last I said, "Mrs. Arnold, did you know that three of my brothers are triplets?" I asked.

Before she could answer, Marilyn jumped into the conversation: "And they don't have to wear name bracelets!"

"No," said Carolyn. "They dress differently. Everyone can tell Mallory's brothers apart."

"Even though they're identical," I added.

"Yes?" said Mrs. Arnold, frowning.

"Well, the thing is," I went on, "I think Marilyn and Carolyn would like to be — "

"Different," spoke up Marilyn. "But we look alike and dress alike, so everyone treats us like one person — the same person."

"And we aren't one person, Mommy!" said Carolyn desperately. "We're *two*. Only no one

101

knows it. At school, the kids call both of us 'Marilyn-or-Carolyn.' "

I cringed, remembering that that was how *I* used to think of the girls.

"We hate it!" added Marilyn.

"The girls do look sweet in their matching outfits," I said, "but," I added quickly as Carolyn poked me in the ribs, "they've told me they think they're old enough to choose their own clothes. They have different tastes."

"If we went to school *look*ing different," said Marilyn, "maybe the kids would get to know who we are."

Oh, good line, I thought as Mrs. Arnold melted before our very eyes.

"Girls," she said, "I never realized. . . . You're so adorable in your matching outfits. And it's so easy to lay out the same clothes for you every day and to buy two of everything. Plus, when you were little you liked looking identical, didn't you?"

"Yes, but we're not babies anymore," said Carolyn. "We can choose our own clothes every day. Honest."

"And if you let us come shopping with you," said Marilyn, "we could pick out the kinds of things we each like."

The twins looked hopefully at their mother.

"Of course you can come shopping with me."

"Can I grow my hair out?" asked Marilyn.

"Can I get mine cut?" asked Carolyn.

"Oh, you two," said Mrs. Arnold with a little gasp, and for a moment I was afraid she was going to cry. "I feel terrible. I always assumed that since your father and I liked the way you look, *you* liked the way you look."

"Well, we used to," Carolyn admitted.

"But not anymore," added her sister.

"Mallory," said Mrs. Arnold, "thank you. I know it wasn't easy for you to bring this to my attention."

"It wasn't," I said with a smile, "but I really like Marilyn and Carolyn. I'm glad this worked out."

"Mallory," whispered Carolyn, nudging me.

"Oh, right," I said. "There's one more thing."

"Yes?" said Mrs. Arnold.

"Mommy," Carolyn began, "you know the money we got for our birthday? Well, if you say it's okay, we want to spend it on new clothes."

"That's okay," agreed Mrs. Arnold quickly. "It's your money."

"Great," I spoke up. "Could I take them

shopping on Thursday? You could drop us off downtown on your way to the school and pick us up afterward."

"Please?" begged the twins.

"It's a date," said Mrs. Arnold.

The girls cheered.

And I walked home that afternoon feeling as if I were on air.

CHAPTER 12

By the time I reached my own house, not only did I feel as if I were on air, but I'd come up with another idea. (I was getting like Kristy Thomas, with all my ideas.) Anyway, the talk with Mrs. Arnold had gone awfully well. So it had occurred to me that I should probably try talking to my own parents. If I really wanted pierced ears and decent hair, maybe I should tell them so, instead of moping around, dropping hints about how unattractive and babyish I thought I was. Mrs. Arnold had given in to an awful lot, and the twins were barely eight years old. Imagine what my parents might agree to for someone who was closer to twelve than eleven.

As soon as I walked through our front door I ran up to my room, hoping Vanessa wouldn't be there. She wasn't. Good. There was about a half an hour before dinner, and I needed peace to plan my strategy. I wanted to talk to

Mom and Dad right after dinner, and I figured I would *need* a good strategy.

It never hurts to be prepared, especially with Mom and Dad. As the parents of eight children, they know every trick in the book — because one or the other of us kids has pulled every trick in the book at least once. My parents can tell a real stomachache from a fake one. They know when someone is eating and when someone is just moving food around on the plate. And I'm pretty sure they have eyes in the backs of their heads — under their hair or something — because without even turning around, they can see a kid who's trying to sneak something upstairs. Maybe they are wizards.

After twenty minutes, the ideal plan of attack came to me: bargaining. I am very good at bargaining. Once, I went to a flea market and saw this really neat old jewelry box. The price tag said $7.50, but I bargained with the guy who was selling it and bought it for $4.75. The man was asking for more than the box was worth, so first I offered *less* than it was worth (only a dollar) and finally we agreed to $4.75, which was a pretty fair price.

Yes, I thought, bargaining just might work.

Dinner that night was a typical Pike meal. Nicky tortured Claire by telling her that in first grade she would get six hours of homework each night and her gym teacher would be Mr. Berlenbach, who would make everyone play touch football whether they wanted to or not.

"That's not true!" cried Claire.

Nicky put his hands over his ears and began humming loudly. "Hmm, hmm-hmm, hmm-hmm. I ca-an't hear you! Hmm, hmm-hmm, hmm-hmm."

Then Adam stuck two straws up his nose and announced that he was a walrus, at which point I said, "Mother, that is revolting." (It couldn't hurt to get on her good side before our talk.)

"It certainly is," she agreed. "Everyone, calm down and behave."

"Everyone?" echoed Margo. "Even Daddy?"

"No, Daddy is behaving himself quite nicely," said my father.

We all laughed. But that didn't stop Jordan from very quietly singing the most disgusting song he knows: "Great big globs of greasy grimy gopher guts, little birdies' dirty feet — "

He stopped abruptly when I kicked him under the table. Margo was turning green, and I didn't want dinner to wind up being such a disaster that Mom and Dad would be too fed up for a talk.

Things calmed down. Margo's face returned to its normal color. We finished our meal. I helpfully volunteered to clean up the kitchen, and I even made coffee for Mom and Dad. I brought it to them in the living room, where they were unwinding.

"Oh, Mallory, you're a lifesaver," said Mom.

"Thanks, honey," added Dad.

"You're welcome. . . . Um, could I talk to you about something?"(Hadn't I said almost the same thing to Mrs. Arnold just a couple of hours earlier?)

My parents glanced at each other, and in that one glance, I could see that they had figured out everything. Their eyes were saying, "Oh, so that's why she was so helpful during dinner, and then cleaned up the kitchen and made coffee for us."

I think they really are wizards.

Wizards or not, I had to go on with my talk. I mean, I'd already said I wanted to talk to them, so I'd better get started.

"Mom, Dad," I began, "I'm — I'm eleven years old. Soon I'll be twelve."

"And after that you'll be a teenager," said Dad, groaning slightly.

"Exactly!" I exclaimed. "I'm not a kid anymore. But I feel like one. I have this dumb hair, and my clothes are sort of, well, babyish.

They're *nice*," I added diplomatically, "but they're young. And I would really like to get my ears pierced." (I had purposely decided not to say, "Half the girls in my class have pierced ears," because then one of my parents would have said, "If half the girls in your class were going to jump off a cliff, would you do that, too?") "I would also like to get contact lenses," I went on. "That's all I want — a haircut, pierced ears, contact lenses, and a brand-new wardrobe." (If I got permission for a haircut, I'd be lucky. But that's how bargaining works.)

"What?" cried my mother with a gasp. "You want *what*?"

"A haircut, pierced ears, contact lenses, and a new wardrobe."

My parents just stared at me. This must have been one trick they hadn't encountered. I decided to try another.

I hung my head. "I'm such a baby," I moaned. "I'm a freak."

"Oh, honey, you are not," said Mom sympathetically.

"You are also not old enough to get contact lenses," added Dad.

"And I'm afraid we can't afford a new wardrobe for you," said my mother. "Do you have any idea how much that would cost?"

I did, but I didn't say so. The wardrobe was one of my bargaining chips. It was something I wasn't expecting at all, so I could easily give it up.

"No," I replied. "How much?"

"A lot," said Dad.

"Oh." I hung my head again.

"I don't see why you couldn't get your hair cut, though," said Mom. "Could you pay for half of it with your baby-sitting money?"

"Sure!" I cried.

"All right. Then you may get your hair cut. On one condition."

"What?" I asked.

"That you don't go to that place where you'll come out with a green mohawk. I want you to go to the salon downtown."

"Deal." (That was no sacrifice. I'd wanted to go to the salon, anyway.)

I paused, thinking. I'd given up the wardrobe and the contacts, but I'd gotten the haircut. What about the pierced ears? "What about piercing my ears?" I asked, and suddenly I forgot about bargaining and tricks. "Please, please, please, please, *please* can I get them pierced? I really want to. Earrings look so pretty, and I promise I won't get more than one hole in each ear, or wear anything weird like, you know, snake fangs. I'll just wear little gold dots, or maybe gold hoops, but tiny ones. Please could I have my ears pierced?"

Another look was exchanged between Mom and Dad, but I couldn't tell what this one meant.

At last Mom said, "I was twelve when I got my ears pierced. You're pretty close to twelve." She turned to Dad. "What do you think?"

"I suppose it's all right — if it's all right with you."

"It's all right with me on three conditions," replied Mom.

Three conditions this time? I guess my wizard parents know how to bargain, too.

"What are the three conditions?" I asked.

"One," Mom answered, "that you pay for the piercing and the earrings yourself."

"Okay," I said.

"Two, that you do everything you're told to prevent infected ears — put alcohol on them, don't change your earrings right away. *Every-thing*."

"Okay."

"And, three, that you *don't* stick to tiny gold earrings. What's the fun of having pierced ears if you can't wear snake fangs every now and then?"

I laughed. "Oh, thanks, you guys! Thank you so much! This is great! I understand about the contacts and the wardrobe. Really. But would it be okay if I spent my baby-sitting money on clothes sometimes?"

"Of course," said Mom. "Just be sensible."

"Oh, I will! I will! Wow! Thanks again. This is awesome! I have to call Jessi and give her the news."

I ran down to the kitchen phone. Jordan and Byron were there making ice-cream sandwiches out of graham crackers and frozen yogurt. (There is no such thing as privacy at my house.) I leaned against the counter and dialed Jessi's number.

Jessi answered the phone herself.

"Hi, it's me," I said in a rush, "and guess what. My parents said I could get my hair cut and my ears pierced."

"You are kidding!"

"Nope. It's the truth. I just had a talk with them."

From across the kitchen I heard Byron say, "Ooh, big deal. Pierced ears."

"SHHH!" I said. "No, not you, Jessi. Byron. My brothers are being pains. And pigs."

"Yeah, piggy-pains," said Jordan, and he and Byron began to laugh uncontrollably.

"Would you please go somewhere else? . . . No, I don't mean you, Jessi. The piggy-pains."

My brothers finally left, and Jessi and I got down to serious business.

"What are you going to do to your hair?" asked Jessi.

"I'm not sure. It's so curly. Maybe something short would be good. Short and fluffy. But not too short. Oh, I don't know."

"Boy," said Jessi, "if you get your hair cut and your ears pierced, I'll really stick out. I'll look like such a baby at club meetings.

"You don't look like a baby *now*," I said honestly.

"Well, I'd still like to get my hair cut and my ears pierced. Just like you."

"Talk to your parents," I suggested. "It worked for me. But be sure you don't say you want those things because I'm getting them. If you do — "

"I know, I know," Jessi interrupted. "Then my parents will say, 'And if Mallory jumped off a cliff, would you do that, too?' "

We both laughed.

"They must learn that at Parent School," said Jessi.

Jessi and I stayed on the phone until we both remembered we had homework to do. Then we got off in a hurry. But for the rest of the evening, the only thing I could really think about was The New Mallory Pike.

CHAPTER 13

Shopping Day!

I was as excited as the twins were. I couldn't wait to go downtown with them. I just knew we were going to have a totally super time. Not only was it going to be fun, but I couldn't wait to see what sorts of things the twins would actually buy. How different would they look? Marilyn had said she wanted to look more grown-up, and Carolyn had said she wanted to look more cool, but that didn't tell me much. The afternoon just might be full of surprises. Also, I had brought along some of my own spending money, in case I saw something that was perfect for The (Soon-to-Be) New Mallory Pike.

Well, the afternoon *was* full of surprises (and fun), and I got my first surprise as soon as I reached the Arnolds' house. The twins were waiting for me outside again — and they were *not* dressed in matching outfits. They were wearing clothes that their mother had bought and that I knew the twins didn't particularly like, but at least the clothes didn't match. The funny thing was that just by wearing non-identical outfits, the girls suddenly seemed less like twins. Their hair and faces were the same as ever, of course, but getting them out of those matching outfits made a world of difference. They looked more like two little girls than two peas in a pod.

"Oh, boy! Shopping time!" cried Carolyn as I approached.

"We can't wait!" added Marilyn.

"Neither can I," I replied as the twins threw themselves at me. "Gosh, you two look great!"

"We got to wear different clothes as soon as you talked to Mommy," Carolyn told me excitedly.

"We wore different pajamas to bed that night," said Marilyn, "and different clothes to school yesterday, and these clothes to school today."

"And you know what?" Carolyn went on.

"What?" I said.

"Right away, the kids at school tried to tell us apart."

"That's great!" I exclaimed. I took each twin by the hand and we walked up the Arnolds' front path.

"Yeah," agreed Marilyn. "Most of the time, they get us wrong, but they haven't called us 'Marilyn-or-Carolyn' for two whole days!"

I led the excited twins inside, where Mrs. Arnold greeted us with a big smile and immediately bustled us down the stairs and right out the garage door and into the car.

"Sorry for the rush," she apologized, "but I've got a lot to do today. Girls, you have your money, don't you?"

"Yes," they replied. They had managed to grab their (identical) pocketbooks as their mother whisked us to the car.

"Good. Then we're on our way."

Ten minutes later, Mrs. Arnold was driving slowly through Stoneybrook's downtown, caught in a small traffic jam. "How about if I let you out up there, by Bellair's?" she asked.

"Perfect," I said.

Bellair's is a department store. It would be a good place to begin our shopping.

"And why don't I pick you up in front of Bellair's in two hours?"

"Okay. We'll be waiting right by that mailbox," I replied, pointing.

Marilyn and Carolyn said good-bye to their mother, leaning over the back of the front seat to plant kisses on her cheek. Then they tumbled out of the car like puppies, and made a dash for the entrance to Bellair's.

I ran after them. "Hey, you guys!" I called breathlessly. "We have to stick together. No running off. I wouldn't want to lose you."

The girls slowed down.

"Okay, what department should we go to first?" I asked.

"Girls' clothing," said Marilyn and Carolyn in one voice, and I realized then that no matter how much the girls wanted to appear different from each other, there were some almost uncanny likenesses about them. They often spoke as one, or picked up on each other's thoughts as they told a story. I wondered whether they could read each other's minds.

"Girls' clothing," I repeated. I checked the store directory. "Second floor," I announced. "Let's go."

"Goody, there's the escalator," said Carolyn. "I just love escalators."

We rode to the second floor and found the girls' clothing department.

"We have a plan," Marilyn told me.

"Yeah," said Carolyn. "Clothes are expensive, and we have *pretty* much birthday money, but not a *lot*."

"So we want to be very careful today,"

Marilyn went on. "We want to see what **we** like at a lot of stores — "

"And how much the things cost," cut in Carolyn.

" — and then we'll decide what to buy and go back and get them."

"That makes sense to me," I told the girls.

So we began looking.

At Bellair's, Marilyn tried on a beautiful pink mohair sweater. I guess she really did want to look more grown-up. Then she checked the price tag.

"A hundred and thirty-five dollars!" she cried.

The sweater went back on the shelf.

Carolyn looked at a neat white sweat shirt with a glittering yellow moon and two stars on the front. "Oh, cool!" she exclaimed. "And I think I can afford it, but I better wait."

Both girls looked at shoes (loafers for Marilyn, high-top sneakers for Carolyn) and immediately realized that any shoes were out of the question. Too expensive. They bypassed the nightgown rack, the underwear table, and a couple of racks of dresses that looked like the stuff their mother would have chosen for them. Then they stopped and looked at pants. I realized I'd never seen them in pants and hoped they could afford them.

"Nice corduroys," said Marilyn.

"Cool jeans," said Carolyn.

Then in the same breath, they added, "We'll come back."

They had pretty much exhausted the girls' clothing department by that time, so I said, "How about going to the Merry-Go-Round? You could probably find some great accessories there."

"What are excorceries?" Marilyn wanted to know.

"Accessories," I repeated. "They're little things to add to an outfit, like jewelry or barrettes or hair ribbons or cute socks."

I could tell by the looks on the girls' faces that the Merry-Go-Round would be our next stop. So we left Bellair's.

The twins fell in love with the Merry-Go-Round, and I couldn't blame them. I'm sort of in love with it myself. The three of us wandered around the store for at least fifteen minutes, calling out things like, "Ooh, look at this unicorn pin," or "Hey, cool, these barrettes are sparkly!" or "Here are knee socks with rows of hearts on them."

Marilyn and Carolyn did their careful looking and planning, but I made a purchase. Two, actually. I couldn't help myself. I found earrings that were perfect for me — and for Jessi.

119

They were tiny studs in the shape of open books. Since we like to read so much, I bought a pair for each of us. Best friends, I thought, should have matching earrings. We wouldn't always have to wear them together, but they'd be nice to own. And Jessi's pair would be a just-because-you're-my-best-friend present. Guess what, though? Both pairs were *pierced*. That's how certain I was that Jessi would be given permission to have her ears pierced, too.

After the Merry-Go-Round, the twins and I went to a sport shop. There the girls priced socks and shirts, and I bought . . . blue push-down socks! I would have to stop buying things, though, or I'd never be able to pay for the ear-piercing and half of my haircut.

"You guys," I said, as we left the sport shop, "we have to meet your mom in a little less than an hour, so I think you better decide what you want to buy, and then go back and get the things. Are you ready to do that?"

"Yes," said Marilyn.

"I think so," said Carolyn.

"Do you need to do some figuring?" I asked them. They looked like they were frantically trying to add prices in their heads. I could practically see their eyeballs whirling around from the effort. "There's a bench. Let's sit down," I suggested.

120

We sat down and I pulled a pad of paper out of my purse. After much discussion and scribbling and adding and subtracting, we went back to Bellair's.

"Clothes first," said Marilyn. "They're more important than excorceries."

In the girls' clothing department Carolyn tried on the "cool jeans" she had seen. "They're a little expensive, but I can wear them with almost all of my shirts and blouses and sweaters," she said sensibly.

Marilyn tried on the corduroys and didn't like them. "I'm more used to skirts and dresses," she admitted. "I don't want any more baby dresses or things with straps, though. I saw a cute pink jeans skirt. Maybe I should try that on. It was grown-up."

Twenty minutes later, we left Bellair's. Marilyn was carrying a bag with the jeans skirt and a ruffly white blouse in it. She had forked over at least three quarters of her money for them, but looked quite pleased and proud. Carolyn was carrying a bag with the jeans and the moon-and-stars sweat shirt in it. The grins on both girls' faces were at least a mile wide.

We went back to the Merry-Go-Round. Marilyn bought the knee socks with the hearts on them ("I'm tired of tights," she explained) and a pair of pink barrettes.

The barrettes were important because the girls had made a decision about their hair. "If Mommy won't let me get my hair cut right away," said Carolyn, "at least we can wear our hair differently."

"I'm going to pull mine back with barrettes," said Marilyn.

"And I'll wear a headband," added Carolyn, who found one she liked at the Merry-Go-Round.

Our last stop was the sport shop. Marilyn was out of money, but Carolyn bought some push-down socks like the ones I'd gotten, except that they were yellow, to match her new sweat shirt.

As we left the sport shop, the girls turned satisfied faces toward me.

"All our money is gone," commented Marilyn, "but we don't care."

"Yeah, we are so lucky," said her sister. "And from now on, when Mommy goes shopping, we'll go with her. We'll never have to wear yucky clothes again."

Don't count on it, I thought, knowing how mothers can be. But Mrs. Arnold *was* going to try to be understanding. I was pretty sure of it.

I looked at my watch. "Ten minutes until

your mother will be back," I said. "What do you want to do?"

"Oh, please," began Carolyn, "could we go to the ladies' lounge in Bellair's and put our new clothes on? Please? Then we could surprise Mommy when we meet her."

I didn't see why not, so we returned to Bellair's and told a sales clerk what we wanted to do. The clerk cut the price tags off of the clothes, and Marilyn and Carolyn did a quick change in the lounge. Then we dashed outside to the mailbox.

No Mrs. Arnold yet. I took a moment to really look at the twins. With their new hairdos, they appeared more different than ever. And, I thought, they seemed to have changed from the terrible, troublesome twins into two sunny little girls whom I could tell apart even when they "matched." I thought back to when I began sitting for them and wondered how I could ever *not* have been able to tell Marilyn from Carolyn. And I remembered what terrors they'd been and how I'd dreaded Tuesday and Thursday afternoons. Now I looked forward to them — but my steady job would be over soon. I hoped Mrs. Arnold would need me to sit sometimes in the future. I'd take care of the troublesome twins any day!

A few minutes later, Mrs. Arnold's car pulled to a stop by the mailbox, and the twins and I scrambled inside. I wish I'd had a camera to capture the expressions on Mrs. Arnold's face when she saw Marilyn and Carolyn. First she looked, well, almost horrified . . . then amazed . . . and finally pleased. I think she liked her daughters' new appearances, but they would take some getting used to.

I knew that the Arnolds, all of them, were going to be just fine.

CHAPTER 14

"Guess what, guess what, guess what!"

"What?" I cried. Jessi's voice was at the other end of our phone, and I had never, and I mean *never*, heard it so excited.

"My parents said I can get my ears pierced!"

"Oh, wow! That is awesome!" I screeched. "Now we can go together!"

At the next meeting of the Baby-sitters Club, Jessi and I told the other girls our news.

Claudia started to laugh. "You won't believe this," she said. "It must be ear-piercing season in Stoneybrook! I just got permission to have another hole pierced in one of my ears!"

"You're kidding!" I cried. "Then we should all have them done at the same time. Where are you going to have your ear done?"

"I'm not sure. . . ."

"Hey," said Kristy, "I've got an idea." (Naturally.)

"We haven't had a club party in awhile.

125

Instead of one, how about if we pay Charlie to drive us out to Washington Mall next Saturday. You three could have your ears pierced at that boutique, and then we could shop and eat lunch and stuff. You want to?"

Of course we did.

"Gosh," said Claud, suddenly looking almost sad, "it's too bad Stacey's not here. She would *love* this. She'd probably have another hole pierced in one of her ears, too."

"Why don't you call her?" suggested Kristy in a gentler-than-usual tone. "At least tell her what we're going to do. I bet she'd want to know. Oh, but, um, well, why don't you call her *after* the meeting so you don't tie up the line?" (The old Kristy again.)

"Okay," agreed Claud glumly. Then she brightened. "Hey, Kristy, Mary Anne, Dawn — are you guys going to ask if you can have your ears pierced, too? You should. It would be fun."

"No way!" exclaimed Kristy. And Mary Anne shook her head. (Dawn shook hers, too, but she looked a little uncertain.)

"My father won't let me," explained Mary Anne, "but we'll definitely come with you," she assured us.

"Yeah. We wouldn't miss it for the world!" said Dawn.

* * *

Five days later, Charlie Thomas was dropping us off at an entrance to Washington Mall. It was eleven o'clock in the morning. "See you at three!" he called as he drove off.

Jessi, Dawn, Mary Anne, Claudia, Kristy, and I practically ran inside. I was so excited that my heart was pounding, and I could hear its beat in my ears.

"What should we do first?" asked Kristy when we were in the center of the mall, surrounded by the stores and restaurants and exhibits.

What were we going to do *first*? Weren't we heading straight for the ear-piercing boutique? I'd waited more than eleven years for this moment. We weren't going to postpone it . . . were we?

I gave Kristy a tortured glance, and she laughed. "Just kidding. Of course we're going to do ears first. Come on, everybody."

We headed for the boutique. On the way, Jessi grabbed my hand.

"I'm getting scared," she said.

"Don't be. I mean, try not to be. I think it's going to be fine. You know, they freeze your ears with this spray before they pierce them, so you don't feel anything. Well, you feel the punch, but it doesn't hurt — "

I stopped. The more I said, the worse Jessi looked.

Claudia noticed her then and exclaimed, "Cheer up! This is fun. We're going malling, you guys. We've never done this as a club!"

Malling. It had a nice ring to it.

Thirty seconds later, the six of us were gathered around the ear-piercing boutique. We were looking at the display of earrings.

"May I help you?" asked a young woman. She was wearing a name tag that read "Sue," and I was relieved to see that it wasn't the same woman Claire had scared to death when she'd screamed, watching the ear-piercing with Margo and me.

My friends looked at me, so I stepped forward. I was feeling pretty calm. I usually am calm. In fact, the more there is to be nervous about, the calmer I become.

"I want to get my ears pierced, please," I told Sue, "and so does she," (I pointed to Jessi), "and she wants one more hole in one ear," I added, indicating Claudia.

"Very good." Sue smiled. "Choose your earrings first. We suggest the simple gold studs, no large hoops or anything fancy."

"Okay," I said.

Jessi and I chose tiny gold balls and Claudia produced an earring she already owned, which

Sue said she could use after it had been sterilized.

"All right. Who's first?" Sue wanted to know.

My friends were grinning. Somebody nudged me forward. "Go on, Mal," said Dawn. "Ear-piercing was your idea."

I hopped onto the stool. In a few minutes, my ears would be pierced. I would look so, so cool. I didn't care what the piercing would feel like.

Sue took a pen and made a tiny mark on each of my earlobes. "Do those look even to you?" she asked. "If they do, that's where I'll make the holes."

I leaned over and examined the marks in a mirror on the counter.

"Perfect," I said.

Then, *spray!* Sue blasted my right ear with something cold. And *punch.* She came at me with that gun, an earring loaded into it like a bullet. *Spray* again. *Punch* again. "All done!" said Sue. The gun had pierced my ears and put the earrings in all at once.

I looked in the mirror. I couldn't believe it. There were my ears, shining with actual ear-rings! I had done it! I felt incredibly cool.

"Who's next?" asked Sue as I slid off the stool.

I was sure Claud would hop onto the stool, since Jessi looked like a nervous wreck while Claud seemed to be your basic cool cucumber. But Claud pushed Jessi forward. I guess she thought it would be better for Jessi to get it over with, so she could stop feeling so nervous.

Reluctantly, Jessi climbed onto the stool and Sue marked her ears. "Hold my hand," she whispered to me, sounding extremely embarrassed.

No problem. I gripped her hand. Jessi squeezed her eyes shut.

Spray, punch! Spray, punch!

Jessi hadn't moved. Her eyes were still closed.

"It's over," I told her.

"You're kidding," she replied. She opened her eyes. "That was nothing!"

"Look at yourself in the mirror," said Sue.

Jessi looked — and grinned.

"Pretty sexy," Mary Anne teased her.

"Okay, Claud, you're on," said Kristy.

Ever so casually, Claudia climbed onto the stool. Sue marked a second spot on one of her ears.

"That looks fine," said Claudia breathily. She folded her hands and sat back. She might have been in a restaurant, waiting for someone to come take her order.

Spray! Punch!

130

"Thanks!" said Claud brightly. She jumped up — then started to slump to the floor.

Kristy and Dawn caught her arms and eased her back onto the stool.

"Put your head between your legs," Sue instructed her briskly.

Claud did as she was told. After a moment, she raised her head.

"Feel better?" asked Sue.

Claudia nodded sheepishly. "I think I can walk now."

"Okay, but just a sec," said Sue. "I have to give all three of you a few instructions on caring for your ears over the next few weeks."

She talked to us about cleaning the holes with alcohol, and not changing the earrings, and turning the posts. Then we paid Sue and left.

"I am so, so embarrassed. I can't believe I almost passed out," wailed Claudia. At the same time Dawn cried, "Wait! I changed my mind. I want my ears pierced after all. I've got to call my mom!"

The next few moments were sort of confusing. Mary Anne sat down on a bench with Claud and tried to make her feel better. Kristy dashed off with Dawn to look for a pay phone, and Jessi and I kept trying to find mirrors or windows in which we could admire our ears.

Five minutes later, Jessi, Dawn, and Kristy gathered at the bench.

"My mom gave me permission!" cried Dawn. "And guess what. She said I could get *two* holes in each ear!"

So we returned to Sue.

Spray, punch, punch! Spray, punch, punch!

When we finally left the ear-piercing boutique for good, we went malling. First, we sort of window-shopped to see what was what. Those of us who had just had our ears pierced were pretty low on money, though.

Then we ate lunch at Burger King. "Lunch is being paid for out of the club treasury," Kristy announced, "since we're malling instead of having a party or a sleepover."

After lunch, we made the rounds of the stores again. Kristy and Mary Anne kept ducking into little shops and making secret purchases. They wouldn't tell the rest of us what they were buying.

We went to the Music Cellar and checked out the new tapes.

Finally, about half an hour before Charlie was supposed to pick us up, we parked ourselves outside of Donut Delite and spied on the cute boys working inside. I have to admit that this was fascinating to Claudia, Dawn,

Mary Anne, and even Kristy, but that Jessi and I couldn't stop looking at our ears in store windows.

Today, I decided, I had taken the first big step toward becoming The New Mallory Pike.

CHAPTER 15

"Order, please!" called Kristy Thomas. It was time for another Monday meeting.

Three weeks and two days had gone by since the Baby-sitters Club's ear-piercing adventure. My steady job with the Arnolds had ended — but already I had sat for the twins twice more, and a weekend job was lined up.

And two days ago, on a red-letter Saturday, a couple of very important things had happened to me, The New Mallory Pike. I had changed my earrings for the first time, and (ta-dah) I had gotten my hair cut!

I have to admit that I looked pretty good, even with my glasses. And even with the revolting braces the orthodontist had put on my teeth a few days earlier.

Jessi had gone with me to the hairdresser. When I entered the salon, I still didn't know exactly what I wanted done. Luckily Amber, the woman who was going to cut my hair, was very understanding.

"I'll show you some pictures," she said. "See what you like. Then I'll tell you if I can do it to your hair."

Jessi and I looked through a book filled with photos of hairstyles. I pointed out four to Amber before she said, "Now *that's* one your hair is perfect for. See how wavy that style is? It's all natural. No perm or anything. When we cut your hair, your curls will relax into those waves."

So here I was, sitting in Claudia's room with my pierced ears (I was wearing the open books I'd bought at the Merry-Go-Round), my fluffy, short hair (which showed off my ears nicely), and, well, my braces. (I tried not to think about the braces too much.)

Kristy was perched in the director's chair, wearing her visor. "Order," she called again.

The rest of us quieted down.

"Well, let's see," Kristy began.

Well, let's see? Our president never opens meetings that way. She always knows just what to say, just what she wants to accomplish. But at the moment, she sounded sort of vague.

"Um," Kristy went on. "Oh, yeah. Has everyone read the notebook?"

"Yes," answered the rest of us in bored voices.

"Well, um. . . . Oh, Dawn, how's the treasury?"

"Still a little low since we went malling, but we have enough to pay Charlie to drive you to and from meetings this week, and after I've collected today's dues" (everyone groaned) "and next Monday's, we'll be okay again."

The six of us fished around for dues money, which we handed to Dawn. She counted it, made a notation on a page in the record book, and placed the money in the treasury envelope.

"Okay, well, oh, yeah," said Kristy. "Any business to discuss?" (It was as if she'd just thought of it. You'd never know she asks us that question at the beginning of absolutely every club meeting.)

I half-raised my hand (how kindergarten of me) and said, "Kristy, is everything all right with you?"

"Oh, sure. Why?"

"I don't know."

"Well, I'm fine."

"Okay."

Kristy paused. "Darn it!" she finally exclaimed. "I can't stand it any longer. Mary Anne, it's time for — "

Ring, ring. I couldn't believe it. The phone! And just when Kristy was about to . . . to do whatever it was she wanted to do.

Claudia took the call, while Mary Anne flipped through the pages in the record book to check the appointment calendar. When Claud hung up, she said, "That was Mrs. Arnold. She needs a sitter for the twins next Thursday afternoon."

"Let's see," said Mary Anne. "Gosh, three of us are free. Kristy, Dawn, and me."

"Hey, Mal," said Dawn, "how *are* the twins these days? I know you ended up liking them, but . . ."

"Oh, you wouldn't believe them," I replied. "They're completely different. Mrs. Arnold finally let Carolyn get her hair cut. It's really cute, shorter than mine. And Marilyn is growing hers out. They never dress the same anymore, and *everyone* can tell them apart, so they're much happier. Whichever one of you gets the job next Thursday will be really surprised. And pleased," I added. "They are not troublesome twins anymore."

After a lot of discussion, Dawn took the job. Then Kristy said, "Okay. Now — "

Ring, ring!

"Aughh!" cried Kristy.

Three more job calls came in, one right after the other.

We are just too popular.

"Now," Kristy tried again, "Mary Anne and I have some surprises."

"Surprises?" repeated Jessi and I at the same time. (Then we had to hook pinkies and say "jinx.")

"Yup." Kristy smiled secretively. "Okay, Mary Anne."

Mary Anne, who was sitting on the end of Claudia's bed, reached down to the floor and hauled up a tote bag. Out of it, she pulled four small boxes. She handed one to Dawn, one to Claudia, one to Jessi, and one to me.

"These are from Kristy and me," she said. "They're presents in honor of the fact that you guys can now change your earrings."

"Oh, wow!" Jessi and Dawn and I exclaimed. "That was so nice of you! Thanks!"

But Claudia started to laugh. "What a coincidence! Wait, don't open them yet." She slid off the bed, opened a drawer in her desk, and removed three small tissue-wrapped packages, one for Dawn, one for Jessi, and one for me.

Well, we had all guessed that the presents were earrings, of course, so I said, "Hold it!

One more!" and gave Jessi a box containing her pair of book earrings. "I'm sorry I don't have anything for you two," I said to Claud and Dawn, "but I got these before I knew you were going to get your ears pierced, too." I'd brought the earrings along, planning to give them to Jessi after the meeting.

Claud, Dawn, Jessi, and I began opening our presents. We opened the ones from Kristy and Mary Anne first.

"These are the things we kept buying at the mall that day," Kristy informed us. Her eyes were shining.

Well, you've never heard such squealing. The earrings had been chosen very carefully, and we were all thrilled. Dawn had been given two pairs, studs in the shape of California (her home state) and others that were gold loops with oranges hanging from them. California oranges, I guess. Claud's earrings looked like artists' palettes, Jessi's were ballet shoes, and mine were horses, since I like to read about them.

"Thank you, thank you!" we kept saying.

Then we opened Claud's earrings. "I made them myself," she announced.

Even if she hadn't said so, we all would have known. And we began laughing nonstop.

Claud had collected little charms and strung together these wild bunches of miniature Coke cans, eyeglasses, forks, animals, you name it, and added feathers and beads.

We put them on immediately, crowding around Claudia's mirror for a look.

"Don't worry," said Claud. "I made a pair for myself. Oh, and all the posts are hypo-allergenic."

"Boy, I sure wish *I* had pierced ears," said Mary Anne wistfully.

"How about the next best thing?" asked Claudia. She produced two more packages — one for Mary Anne, one for Kristy. They were earrings like the others Claud had made, but they were for nonpierced ears. Kristy and Mary Anne beamed.

"Whoa, it's six o'clock," said Kristy suddenly, and the meeting broke up, the six of us still calling thank you to one another.

Not until Jessi and I were outside and walking down the Kishis' driveway did I say, "Hey, Jessi, you didn't open — "

"I know," she interrupted me. "For some reason, I wanted to do it in private." She pulled my present out of her purse, and we stopped while she tore the paper off the box. "Ooh," she breathed as she peered inside, "books. Just like yours." She paused. "So we can be twins?" she asked.

We both laughed, thinking of Marilyn and Carolyn.

"No," I replied. "Best friends."

"Oh. Best friends," Jessi repeated, and gave me a big hug.

Then we headed for our homes.

Dear Reader:

When I was young, I thought it would be fun to have an identical twin sister. A popular TV show then was *The Patty Duke Show*, about a teenage girl and her cousin growing up in Brooklyn. Patty and Cathy were identical. They looked so much alike that they were able to fool people. I knew several sets of twins, including my cousins Lyman and Jimmy, but none of them were identical. They couldn't get away with what Patty and Cathy could on the show. So I created twins who could — Marilyn and Carolyn Arnold. In fact, I like identical twins so much that I put a set in the Baby-sitters Little Sister series, and the newest member of the Baby-sitters Club is a twin, too. Who knows what kind of trouble Abby and her sister, Anna, will get into?

Happy reading,

Ann M Martin

Ann M. Martin

About the Author

ANN MATTHEWS MARTIN was born on August 12, 1955. She grew up in Princeton, NJ, with her parents and her younger sister, Jane.

Although Ann used to be a teacher and then an editor of children's books, she's now a full-time writer. She gets the ideas for her books from many different places. Some are based on personal experiences. Others are based on childhood memories and feelings. Many are written about contemporary problems or events.

All of Ann's characters, even the members of the Baby-sitters Club, are made up. (So is Stoneybrook.) But many of her characters are based on real people. Sometimes Ann names her characters after people she knows, other times she chooses names she likes.

In addition to the Baby-sitters Club books, Ann Martin has written many other books for children. Her favorite is *Ten Kids, No Pets* because she loves big families and she loves animals. Her favorite Baby-sitters Club book is *Kristy's Big Day*. (By the way, Kristy is her favorite baby-sitter!)

Ann M. Martin now lives in New York with her cats, Gussie and Woody. Her hobbies are reading, sewing, and needlework — especially making clothes for children.

Notebook Pages

This Baby-sitters Club book belongs to _____ .

I am _____ years old and in the _____

grade.

The name of my school is _____ .

I got this BSC book from _____ .

I started reading it on _____ and

finished reading it on _____ .

The place where I read most of this book is _____ .

My favorite part was when _____ .

If I could change anything in the story, it might be the part when

_____ .

My favorite character in the Baby-sitters Club is _____ .

The BSC member I am most like is _____

because _____ .

If I could write a Baby-sitters Club book it would be about ___

_____ .

#21 Mallory and the Trouble with Twins

Carolyn and Marilyn Arnold are identical twin sisters. The person that I look like the most is _____.

One person I don't look anything like is _____.

The two friends I have who look the most like identical twins are _____. Two of my friends who look nothing at all alike are _____.

If I could choose to look like any of my friends, I would want to look like _____. If I could choose to look like any movie or TV star, I would choose to look like _____.

Not all twins are identical; people can be twins without even looking alike! If I could have anyone for a twin sister, I would want it to be _____. If I could have anyone for a twin brother, I would want it to be _____.

The two people I know who would make the worst set of twins are _____.

Age 2 —
Already
a fan of
reading

Age 10 —
Still a fan.
Waiting to
meet my
favorite
author.

SCRAPBOOK

Two of my favorite things—babysitting and Ben.

My family—all ten of us!

Read all the books
about **Mallory**
in the Baby-sitters Club series
by Ann M. Martin

THE BABY-SITTERS CLUB®

The best friends you'll ever have!

Collect 'em all!

by Ann M. Martin

More titles...

The Baby-sitters Club titles continued...

☐ MG48222-X	#78	Claudia and the Crazy Peaches	$3.50
☐ MG48223-8	#79	Mary Anne Breaks the Rules	$3.50
☐ MG48224-6	#80	Mallory Pike, #1 Fan	$3.50
☐ MG48225-4	#81	Kristy and Mr. Mom	$3.50
☐ MG48226-2	#82	Jessi and the Troublemaker	$3.50
☐ MG48235-1	#83	Stacey vs. the BSC	$3.50
☐ MG48228-9	#84	Dawn and the School Spirit War	$3.50
☐ MG48236-X	#85	Claudi Kishli, Live from WSTO	$3.50
☐ MG48227-0	#86	Mary Anne and Camp BSC	$3.50
☐ MG48237-8	#87	Stacey and the Bad Girls	$3.50
☐ MG22872-2	#88	Farewell, Dawn	$3.50
☐ MG22873-0	#89	Kristy and the Dirty Diapers	$3.50
☐ MG22874-9	#90	Welcome to the BSC, Abby	$3.50
☐ MG22875-1	#91	Claudia and the First Thanksgiving	$3.50
☐ MG22876-5	#92	Mallory's Christmas Wish	$3.50
☐ MG22877-3	#93	Mary Anne and the Memory Garden	$3.99
☐ MG22878-1	#94	Stacey McGill, Super Sitter	$3.99
☐ MG45575-3		Logan's Story Special Edition Readers' Request	$3.25
☐ MG47118-X		Logan Bruno, Boy Baby-sitter Special Edition Readers' Request	$3.50
☐ MG47756-0		Shannon's Story Special Edition	$3.50
☐ MG47686-6		The Baby-sitters Club Guide to Baby-sitting	$3.25
☐ MG47314-X		The Baby-sitters Club Trivia and Puzzle Fun Book	$2.50
☐ MG48400-1		BSC Portrait Collection: Claudia's Book	$3.50
☐ MG22864-1		BSC Portrait Collection: Dawn's Book	$3.50
☐ MG48399-4		BSC Portrait Collection: Stacey's Book	$3.50
☐ MG47151-1		The Baby-sitters Club Chain Letter	$14.95
☐ MG48295-5		The Baby-sitters Club Secret Santa	$14.95
☐ MG45074-3		The Baby-sitters Club Notebook	$2.50
☐ MG44783-1		The Baby-sitters Club Postcard Book	$4.95

Available wherever you buy books...or use this order form.

Scholastic Inc., P.O. Box 7502, 2931 E. McCarty Street, Jefferson City, MO 65102

Please send me the books I have checked above. I am enclosing $_____
(please add $2.00 to cover shipping and handling). Send check or money order–no cash or C.O.D.s please.

Name _____ Birthdate_____

Address _____

City_____ State/Zip _____

Please allow four to six weeks for delivery. Offer good in the U.S. only. Sorry, mail orders are not available to residents of Canada. Prices subject to change.

THE BABY-SITTERS CLUB®

by Ann M. Martin

Collect and read these exciting BSC Super Specials, Mysteries, and Super Mysteries along with your favorite Baby-sitters Club books!

BSC Super Specials

BSC Mysteries

More titles ➡